THERE IS BUT ONE

Gina and Charles Martin are young and passionately in love. Their marriage is perfect until Gina learns that she cannot have children. Her husband's failure to understand the effect this has on her precipitates a need for a baby which grows into an obsession. Gradually the young couple's relationship deteriorates until they are little more than strangers and their intense love little more than a memory. Gina hopes first to adopt a baby, then to foster a child, before she seeks a solution outside the law, leading to an unexpected and moving conclusion.

THERE IS BUT ONE

There Is But One

by

Patricia Robins

Dales Large Print Books
Long Preston, North Yorkshire,
BD23 4ND, England.

British Library Cataloguing in Publication Data.

Robins, Patricia
    There is but one.

    A catalogue record of this book is
    available from the British Library

    ISBN   978-1-84262-532-3 pbk

First published in Great Britain in 1965
by Hurst & Blackett Ltd.

Copyright © 1965 by Patricia Robins

Cover illustration © Melvyn Warren-Smith by arrangement
with P.W.A. International Ltd.

The moral right of the author has been asserted

Published in Large Print 2007 by arrangement with
Claire Lorrimer

Dales Large Print is an imprint of Library Magna Books Ltd.

Printed and bound in Great Britain by
T.J. (International) Ltd., Cornwall, PL28 8RW

Prologue

It was raining hard. Mrs Oliver was in the kitchen making the Christmas puddings. The three children were playing in the front room – or they had been playing. Now, as usual, the two daughters were quarrelling.

'Gina, getting over-excited again!' thought her mother disapprovingly. Gina was red haired and had a temper to match. Myra, three years her senior, was placid but a bit inclined of late to be bossy.

'I'm not going to be the child – I want to be the mother!'

Gina's six-year-old voice was piercingly sharp.

'Well, you just can't. You're the smallest, isn't she, Mark?' Myra's tones were deeper and maddeningly superior.

But even as she spoke, Myra knew she had made a mistake appealing to the boy. At nine, Mark always tried his hardest to avoid being dragged into the sisters' quarrels, but when put on a spot, he invariably sided with Gina. Myra didn't understand why and when she stopped to think about it, thought it grossly unfair. However, her mother nearly always sided with her so it was about

7

even in the long run.

'Well, it is her *turn* to be Mother!'

Mark's voice was hesitant but sufficient for Gina, who flung her arms round him and grinned at him happily, then stuck out her tongue to her older sister.

'There! It's my turn. If you don't want to be the child, you can be the nurse. Lots of rich children have nurses. We'll use one of my dolls for a baby.'

Myra scowled and put her head on one side considering. She might appeal to Mother – but Mother when she was busy cooking, often refused to sort out squabbles. Well, she certainly wasn't going to be a silly old nurse.

'I'm not going to play!' she announced, tossing her dark hair back from her round, rosy face. 'I think it's a silly game, anyway. It's – it's babyish!'

Gina's face was a mask of fury. She stamped her foot and glared at Myra, wishing she dared hit her.

'It's not silly and it's not babyish. How, stupid, can it be a baby game when it's playing at grown-ups? It isn't silly, is it, Mark?'

Mark shifted uncomfortably from one foot to another. He adored Gina with a nine-year-old's first uncritical love. But he wished she wouldn't get so worked up about things. Myra was bossy. He wouldn't have come over to their house to play nearly so often if there'd only been Myra – but there was

8

never any peace with Gina – or certainly not for long and sometimes he felt instinctively a very masculine desire for what his father called 'a bit of peace and quiet'.

'Mark 'n me'll jolly well play without you!' Gina was shouting. 'We don't need you in the game anyway.'

She turned to Mark and the angry expression left her face; she looked sparkling and excited. He was ready to fall in now with whatever she suggested.

'You're the father!' she told him. 'And you're coming home from the office and you're very surprised when you open the front door and see me standing there with a baby in my arms. And you say: "Goodness me, is that our new baby!" and I say, "Yes" and you ask if it's a boy or a girl...'

Myra, who had pulled out a painting book and was pretending to be busy painting, said scornfully:

'Don't be silly, Gina. If you have a baby, you have to go to hospital!'

'You don't!' Gina retorted automatically. But she wasn't sure and her tone of voice gave her sister a momentary advantage.

'Yes, you do. I saw a film about it and you didn't – you weren't allowed to go. It was the little film which came after "Snow White" and the mother went to a hospital to have her baby, so there.'

Gina bit her lip angrily. She wanted the

make-believe game to be real – it was her favourite game and she played it with endless permutations, alone, if Myra or Mark or one of her little friends were not there to play with her. She was doll-mad, her mother said, but then her mother didn't know that it wasn't really *dolls* she liked – it was just the nearest she could get until she was grown-up to having a real live baby. She was very maternal.

Suddenly she remembered their neighbour; not Mark's mother who lived on their right, but Mrs Green, on their left.

'What about her!' she shouted triumphantly. 'She had a baby at home. Mother took us in to see it. You didn't go because you were in quarantine for measles. So there!'

She turned back to Mark and told him:

'Go on, Mark. Mind you look very surprised because I've been keeping it a secret 'cos it's your birthday…'

'Stupid!' Myra's voice interrupted Gina again. 'You can't keep babies a surprise.'

'Why not?' Curiosity had overcome irritation.

'I'm not going to tell you!' Myra said, making the most of her superior knowledge. 'You'll have to ask Mother.'

Gina swung round to Mark.

'You tell me!' she commanded. 'Go on, Mark, tell me!'

But the fact was, Mark did not know. Neither his mother nor Gina's were sufficiently modern enough in outlook to approve of young children being given the facts of life too young. Myra had not, in fact, been told anything by her mother but by a school friend who happened to be Mrs Green's older daughter.

'Mum's huge!' Sylvia had confided. 'And she'll go on getting huger until the baby's born.'

Not even Myra had realized why. Privately she had made up her mind not to be greedy like Mrs Green and other mothers when she had a baby. She certainly had no intention of getting so fat.

'Well, aren't you going to tell me?' Gina was insisting.

'I – I don't know!' Mark protested feebly. 'Can't we play something else, Gina?'

Instinct warned her not to push Mark too far. Experience had already taught her that if Mark began to get bored with Mothers and Fathers, there was a next-best game he'd always play.

'All right!' she agreed. 'We'll play Brides and Grooms!'

Mark enjoyed this game. Gina would put a white curtain net over her red gold curls and on top, a silver paper crown. Then she would hold his hand and Myra would thump out on the piano what they all supposed was the wedding march before putting on a white overall back to front and one of her father's collars round her neck and read the marriage service out of the prayer book.

One day, Mark knew, he would be grown up and Gina would really marry him. Then he would take her away to live in a castle and they would keep hundreds of pet animals and, if Gina still wanted them so much, hundreds of babies. They would all have red hair and grey eyes like Gina – but without her quick temper.

For a little while the new game kept the three of them quiet. Then Gina broke into the middle of the marriage service, much to Myra's annoyance, to say:

'I ought to have a bridesmaid. I'll get Lucy – she's my prettiest doll. We can prop her up against the chair and put the end of my veil in her hands so it looks as if she's holding it…'

But Myra refused to go on with the game if there was to be an interruption and while he was waiting for the two of them to fight it out, Mark heard his mother calling him back to tea.

The girls broke off the quarrel to watch him put on his mac and gumboots and disappear into the rain. Gina, more than Myra, felt suddenly deeply depressed. There would be no more Brides and Grooms and no more Mothers and Fathers today – not without Mark. You had to have a real boy to be Father – girls never looked real. To hide her depression, she said to Myra:

'Mark likes me better than he likes you!'

'I don't care!'

'He's going to marry me when I'm big enough.'

Myra shrugged. She wasn't very interested in Mark. She preferred the company of her two school friends, Jane and Esther. Most of all, she preferred to be with her mother in the kitchen, helping to cook. She loved cooking and knew that her mother approved of her being what she called 'so domesticated'. Mother didn't approve nearly so much of Gina's passion in life – dolls. It was all right when Gina was just playing with dolls but somehow, her young daughter didn't seem able to keep imagination and reality apart. She would lose herself in some imaginary situation and, as she did with everything else, carry it to extremes.

Last week there'd been the doll Lucy episode. Gina had pretended she was ill. That was all right until teatime, when Gina had flatly refused to move from the doll's cot.

'I mustn't leave her. I'm her mother!'

'Come along this minute, Gina!' Her mother had been cross.

'But I can't. She might die while I'm having tea. She's very, very ill. The doctor said she mustn't be left for a moment. Her temperature is two hundred and eight.'

'Gina!'

'But, Mother, Lucy's ill...'

Ill or not, Gina had been sent up to her bedroom where she had sobbed her heart out. Myra, a little uneasily, heard her screams and wasn't sure with whom her sympathy lay. Of course, Gina ought to be obedient to Mother and yet – well, you could tell from Gina's crying that she really believed Lucy was going to die!

Myra was very practical. She accepted that Gina was different from herself and in a way, was fond of her younger sister. She would have been a deal fonder if Gina had been a little less strong-willed and easier to boss. Myra liked telling people what to do. But she genuinely admired Gina who was inventive and amusing and she wasn't in the least jealous of her young sister's vivacious charm and good looks which invariably brought forth compliments from neighbours and relatives who didn't know what a passionate, one-track-minded child she could be.

The friendship between the sisters and the boy next door continued into their teens. Both families took it for granted that one day Gina and Mark would marry. It was only Myra who doubted it. Herself engaged at nineteen to a stock-broker, she said to her sister:

'I suppose any day now Mark will propose to you, Gina. You aren't going to say "yes", are you?'

Gina looked up at her elder sister with mischievous grey eyes.

'I might! Why, what have you got against Mark?'

Myra shrugged her shoulders.

'I've nothing at all against Mark – except that he is far too weak with you. You need someone to *manage* you, Gina – someone to sweep you off your feet. I think you take advantage of Mark's adoration but that you don't return it.'

Gina's face turned a shade pinker. For once, her sister Myra was very near the truth. She loved Mark but she wasn't 'in love' with him – not in the way heroines were 'in love' in the novels she now read avidly. There was no excitement in going out with Mark – just a quiet pleasant understanding and, as Myra had so shrewdly guessed, a sop to her vanity because Mark did so adore her.

Sometimes, at night, she would dream of a handsome unknown stranger who'd hold out his arms and she, with absolute certainty, would float, wraithlike, into his embrace. It was never that way with Mark. He would kiss her good night after a dance or if they had been to the cinema, holding her close but carefully, as if she might break. She liked his kisses which were gentle and controlled, but they never stirred her as she was stirred in her dreams by the unknown stranger.

15

Because she was a romantic, she was disappointed in Myra's choice of a husband. Malcolm was nice enough but without a shred of glamour. Gina could not see what her sister found so marvellous about him. But then, she and Myra had seldom agreed about anything except that they both wanted to get married and have large families. Myra saw herself as a housewife, efficient manager and utterly content in her domestic setting. Gina saw herself as a combination of lover to her husband and mother to her large family of babies. She was a strange mixture of the romantic and the maternal.

Myra, having obtained a domestic science degree at school, was now teaching domestic science. Gina worked in a nearby large suburban store as a salesgirl. She quite enjoyed the company of the other girls and the contact with the public with whom she got on well. One day, she was sure, the stranger of her dreams would come into the shop and that is how they would meet. She spent a lot of time day-dreaming, imagining why a young attractive bachelor might come into the soft-furnishing department where she worked.

But strangely enough, it was through the plump, placid Malcolm that she and Charles first met. Charles Martin was one of the ushers at Malcolm's wedding.

Gina had recognized him at once as the

man in her dreams. He, too, seemed to recognize her for he came over to her as soon as he could at the reception and asked if they had not met somewhere before. From then on, she had forgotten poor Mark, waiting patiently in the background for her to finish her conversation with Charles and go and talk to him. It was with Charles she had finished up the evening – not Mark. Mark kept in the background and never tried to interfere in the friendship that developed and progressed so swiftly as the evening wore on.

For Gina, the party that followed Myra's wedding was like one of her dreams come true. As the only bridesmaid she should, of course, have had the first dance with the best man, but Charles had swept her on to the floor before the best man had finished eating. He had monopolized her with a strong determination that had excited Gina. By the end of the evening, she knew that for the first time in her life, she was really in love.

Mark must have known it, too, for he kept away from the house the following weeks. But Gina was too happy, too much in love, even to notice his absence. It wasn't until three weeks later when Charles asked her to marry him that she remembered poor Mark and went first to tell him the news.

'I'm so sorry, Mark. I – know when we were children we sort of promised each other that one day we … well, that it was understood that you and I...'

'Forget it, Gina. I think I always knew that you would never marry me. I quite understand. I can understand why you're in love with Charles – he's a nice fellow. You don't have to explain anything to me.'

'But we'll stay friends, won't we, Mark?'

'Of course, if that's what you want. When are you getting married, Gina?'

Suddenly, with Mark's question, the whole whirlwind courtship became real and Gina caught her breath at the wonder of it.

'Soon, if we can. But I'm still only seventeen and I think Mother and Father will insist on our waiting at least a year. Oh, Mark, I'm so happy.'

Thinking back to this conversation, she realized that she had probably been unintentionally cruel to Mark by letting him see how much in love she was. But there was little point in prevarication. She loved Charles and he loved her and as soon as she could persuade her parents to agree, they were going to be married. She consoled herself with the thought that she had never made any promises to Mark and that he had never really expected her to marry him.

Her parents were disappointed. They liked Charles well enough but they, like so many people who had seen Mark and Gina constantly together, had taken it for granted that Gina would marry Mark. When Myra returned from her honeymoon, she met Charles and afterwards told her sister:

'Well, you won't be able to boss *him* around the way you do poor old Mark. You've met your match, Gina – in more ways than one!'

Other people's remarks failed to touch Gina deeply. Her mind, thoughts and heart were too full of Charles.

'We're going to be so happy, darling!' Charles told her over and over again, confidently and sweepingly. 'We'll buy a little cottage in the country near my iron works and I'll work terribly hard and we'll be very rich.'

Gina laughed happily.

'I don't care if we aren't rich. All I want is to be with you.'

'Well, I care – I mean to make a lot of money so I can give you anything in the world you want!'

'But Charles, I don't want anything – except you, and, of course, a family. You do like children, don't you, darling?'

'Of course I do. But not right away. At first I want you all to myself. I'm a possessive type as you'll find out. Which reminds me, Gina, what about this fellow, Mark. Do you have to see so much of him? He always seems to be hanging round your house.'

'Well, he lives next door!' Gina had laughed, and then added more seriously: 'You don't have to be jealous of Mark. He's my best friend, but I could never fall for

19

him. I'm just very, very fond of him.'

'Your mother said you and he were child-hood sweethearts!'

'It wasn't really like that!' Gina told him. 'Mark and I went out together a lot – I liked him better than any other boy I knew. But we weren't engaged – in fact, Mark never talked about being in love. It was only when we were children we used to pretend in games that we were married – you know, darling, how kids play at "weddings" and at "Mothers and Fathers".'

'I think he's in love with you, poor devil!' Charles could afford to be generous for he knew Gina loved him and only him.

She felt momentarily guilty but when Charles took her into his arms, there was no room for thoughts of Mark or anyone else.

'Let's get married soon, soon!' Charles whispered passionately against her soft hair.

But it was eighteen months before in fact he married her. At first, Gina's parents had insisted they wait until Gina's eighteenth birthday, and then Charles had been unable to find the cottage he wanted. But Gina hadn't minded the waiting. She had gone on with her job, saving money now so that they could furnish their dream cottage when they found it. And there was Myra's baby – a darling little boy they called Robert. All Gina's maternal instincts rushed to the fore when she saw her tiny nephew and she thought longingly of the children she and Charles would have – not at once – she agreed with Charles that at first they would want only each other.

She saw less and less of Mark as the days and weeks rushed by. When she was not with Charles, she was with Myra and the baby, helping to bath and feed him and take him out for walks in the pram. She was perfectly happy and although she longed for the wedding day to be finally fixed, the waiting was not too hard for her; not so hard as it was for Charles who was older and experienced and who wanted Gina with a young man's impatient desire for complete possession.

Sometimes he would go with her to visit Myra. Malcolm was an old school friend and although the two men had never been very close, Malcolm had asked him to be an usher at his wedding and because of it, he had met Gina and therefore felt grateful to his future brother-in-law. He enjoyed their weekends with the young married couple, charmed by Gina's sweet attentions to the baby, and hiding what he knew to be a childish jealousy of her interest in it. One day they would have kids of their own, he told himself, and then he would sit and watch her ministering to them with nothing but pride. And deep down he knew that Gina was as much in love with him as he was with her. Driving her home, she would nestle against him, like a child herself, perfectly responsive to his moods and thoughts and returning his kisses and caresses with a warm-hearted, even wild, passion that excited and pleased him. He never ceased to wonder that this beautiful passionate girl should have sprung from such a family. Myra was bordering on plain; was quiet and placid and unremarkable. Gina's parents were suburban – even a little old-fashioned and stuffy and neither could ever have been more than nice-looking. Yet Gina was a glowing, vivacious girl, intelligent, sweet, highly strung perhaps, but never, never dull or drab. She was everything he had ever wanted in a woman and because she represented perfection, he wanted to give her perfection. For this reason alone did he put off the wedding until he had found the perfect little house to which he could take his young bride.

They honeymooned in Capri and returned home more in love than ever. As he carried Gina over the threshold of their first home together, the sun shone down on them and Charles whispered:

'Everything will always be perfect for us, my darling wife. How lucky we are!'

And with shining eyes, Gina sighed contentedly and endorsed his words.

'The luckiest couple in the whole wide world.'

And so their marriage began.

1

The train was nearly empty. Gina had the carriage to herself. The early edition of the *Evening Standard* lay unopened on her lap as the train chugged its way slowly down the branch line to Hartfield and the Sussex countryside where she lived.

The guard, coming in to clip her ticket and break her solitude, gave her a brief curious glance. She was pretty enough; short, reddish brown curls and grey eyes, but no prettier than a lot of girls he saw nowadays. They all wore quite a bit of make-up and dressed in smart clothes, like this girl's blue tweed suit. It was her expression, really, that had made him give her a second glance. She looked so desperately unhappy.

'All right, miss?' he asked, hesitating a moment before leaving her alone again. In his thirty years on the railways, he'd seen three suicides. He was due to retire in a month's time and he didn't want another nasty turn to end up with.

Gina gave him a sudden warm smile.

'I'm fine, thank you!'

After he had gone, she leaned back in the corner seat and stared out of the window without seeing the quickly passing view. She thought:

'I must learn to conceal my feelings a bit better. Even a stranger noticed something is wrong. I mustn't let Charles know how miserable I am. Oh, Charles, I wish you were here… I wish your arms were round me and I could cry and cry…'

The first shock of the bad news was wearing off. The full impact of pain was hitting her hard.

'No baby!' the specialist had said. *'So sorry, Mrs Martin … but you did ask for the truth…'*

Yes, she'd paid five guineas for the privilege of a Harley Street specialist's opinion and she'd wanted the truth. But she'd never really believed it could be so awful, so final.

Her thoughts went back over the past year of her marriage to Charles. They'd been so perfectly, unbelievably happy together. If anything, they were even more in love now than the bright, sunny day they were married in the village church.

'Charles!' she thought now with an ache of longing. So far they had only shared happiness but she never doubted that it would halve the pain for her if she could share this with him, too. Somehow he would make it seem less awful, less frightening.

No baby … neither this year nor next nor ever. She and Charles could never have children. Yet they talked so often about the family they wanted – two boys and two girls, with about five years between each pair.

'Then the girls will appreciate their brothers' boyfriends when they are grown up!' Charles had said smiling.

Gina thought of Charles smiling and knew that in her imagination both their sons were like him. He was very handsome. It wasn't just a case of 'rose-coloured spectacles'. Her mother, her married sister, Myra, and her friends, all thought him very good-looking.

He was just a breath over six foot tall, lean, long-legged, with dark, almost black hair and bright hazel eyes set in a strong tanned face. There was nothing effeminate about Charles. He not only looked strong but he had a forceful personality. He knew what he wanted and he usually got it.

Gina smiled to herself remembering how Charles had symbolically bombed his way into her life, breaking up the association with poor old Mark – Mark who had been her childhood's sweetheart. But Charles had been so devastatingly attractive, she had found herself being rushed into an engagement three weeks after their first meeting. Georgina became 'my Gina' to Charles. His lovely grey-eyed, red-haired Gina. He had always been attracted by that shade of red in a woman's hair, he had told her; that deep burning colour, like a flame. It was perfect with her magnolia skin, her dark narrow brows and heavy lashes. She was beautiful enough, he said, to be a film star.

She was his ideal.

His vitality, his drive, fascinated Gina. As a business man he was soon a success.

He bought up a small run-down wrought-iron factory near Brighton and in two years had built it up into a thriving affair making sufficient profit to keep them both comfortably, if not in luxury. They had bought a small cottage off the beaten track in Sussex. They ran a Morris Minor and could afford a daily woman to do the cleaning. Gina liked to do the actual cooking herself. She was perfectly happy in her small kitchen, surrounded by pots, pans and two or three cooking books. Charles called her his 'Cordon Bleu'.

They were very, very happy.

For a moment, Gina closed her eyes as she remembered the passionate love-making that they shared so often and which seemed to colour everything they did together. However wonderful their day, it was always the night that brought them perfect completion. The honeymoon ecstasies seemed to go on and on. Charles was a good lover and she had learned never to reach satiety.

Gina was sure no other couple were as happy as she and Charles.

Once she had said to her mother:

'It's too good to be true – something awful will happen!'

But she didn't really believe it. As long as she and Charles had each other, nothing 'awful' could touch them. She was confident that she was living with Charles in a magic circle of love that protected them from the 'slings and arrows.'

She felt sorry for her sister. Myra's husband was short, plump and placid. Gina liked Malcolm well enough – he was kind to Myra and an excellent father to their two children; but he was so dull, so unromantic compared with Charles. Gina felt sure that Myra and Malcolm could never possibly reach the heights of love to which she and Charles had climbed in such dizzy fashion.

There was only one thing she envied Myra – her two children. Robert was two and adorable, and Betsy-Ann nine months old, a beauty already with Gina's red hair and smoky-grey eyes.

'Come on, Gina!' Myra would tease Gina in her usual blunt way. 'When are you and Charles going to produce a couple of cousins for my kids?'

Gina protested. For the first six months of their marriage, she hadn't really wanted a baby. She lived only for Charles. But lately, she knew that she had begun to want a child, badly. A baby would be the right and perfect outcome of their shared passion.

'I've no objection if you really want an infant,' Charles had told her when she brought up the subject to him. 'After all, you're the one who will have to produce it and look after it. And you make sure it won't spoil that lovely figure of yours. A good doctor and modern treatment for you, my love!'

Then Gina was sure that a baby was what she must have.

Before she married Charles there had never seemed to be enough time in each day to see to all the things she wanted to do. It was a rush to get her hair done, her nails varnished, her clothes pressed and mended; to see a new film at the local, or fit in a game of tennis with Mark, as well as the twice-a-week dances and the Cordon Bleu cookery classes she tried to squeeze into her schedule.

Now she had stopped work. Charles had insisted. His wife was not going out to any job. He didn't like the idea – so time for Gina took on a new aspect.

At first it had been bliss to linger over all the household jobs. There were curtains to make for the cottage, the spare room to be painted, shelves to be papered; and later on, jam to be made and fruit bottled.

In her spare time she had had a chance at last to read books; to do some sewing; to go out for a walk and linger round the shops and buy wonderful bargains at the local sales. Gradually everything fell into place. Time started to drag.

Charles often worked late, to get his business on to its feet. He went off early, just before eight. He was rarely back before seven at night. Gina began to spend most of her afternoons with Myra. She loved looking after Robert and her tiny prototype, Betsy-Ann. Luckily for the sisters they both had settled in Sussex, Gina in her old cottage, Myra in a modern bungalow. Malcolm was more thrifty and less artistic in type than Charles. A bungalow in his opinion was more of a commercial proposition and cheaper to run than one of those old places.

In Myra's busy home there was always so much to do – ironing, children's meals, tidying up their toys, bringing in or putting out the pram and the hanging out or folding up of the baby's nappies. Invariably, Gina would glance at her watch and say:

'Goodness, Myra, it's after six. I'll have to rush!'

Days spent at home seemed endless as the hands of the clock inched their way cautiously round from three – to four – to five – to six, and at long last to seven when the sound of a car, the familiar whistle outside the door meant that Charles was home.

Gina was crazy about the weekends with Charles. They seemed literally to be swallowed up at a gulp. Then it was Monday and Charles would be gone again, and Gina left with only the daily woman for company,

29

unless she went over to the bungalow.

A baby was the obvious answer. Gina loved her niece and nephew so much that she was bound to love her own children, much more. She began to wait eagerly for the first signs of pregnancy. But nothing happened.

The months went by, and each time, failure stared her in the face and seemed a little harder to bear.

Charles was aggravatingly unconcerned.

'Not to worry – plenty of time, darling. Don't get so het up about it. Why, we've only been married a few months.'

But soon it was a year. Myra said:

'Why not go and see my gynaecologist, Ginny? Remember I went to him after I had Robert and felt so ill? He was wonderful – awfully sympathetic as well as clever. If he tells you all is well, you can go home and relax. I'm sure half your trouble is that you're so tensed up – trying too hard, or something, I'd say.'

At first, Gina refused. She did think of going to her local National Health doctor but somehow it didn't seem right to bother such a busy man with nothing more than her tale of woe – a tale, really, of anxiety rooted in her intense desire for mother-hood. In the end, she decided to take Myra's advice and go to Naughton-Irving – Myra's specialist. If *he* said everything was normal, she could stop being afraid. She could sit back placidly and wait.

Today in that train her hands tightened round the newspaper on her lap. The train stopped for a few minutes at one of the stations – then jerked forward again.

'No baby!' she thought. She was cold with horror and still not fully credulous of the facts. Mr Naughton-Irving had said something about her particular condition occurring in only one in a hundred thousand women. A rare malformation – and not even an operation could put it right. *One in a hundred thousand!*

'But why me? Why *me?*' Gina asked herself, fighting desperately against the injustice of life.

She realized suddenly that she had quite unwittingly cheated Charles. He wanted children too. He had been willing to wait – but not to do without them altogether. He was very fond of young Robert and Betsy-Ann. His 'baby Lollo' he called Gina's red-haired niece. With some other woman, he could have had children, but with her … she ought never to have married him.

'Oh, Charles!' She felt sick with anxiety and misery. How could she tell him – yet she must do so. Would he change once he knew that she wasn't after all a whole and complete woman?

'You should get in touch with one of the Adoption Societies and adopt a baby!' the specialist

had said.

A crumb of comfort. But it was Charles' children she had wanted so much – two little boys at first who looked exactly like their father. She wanted her own daughters, too – not someone else's...

Then she thought of Robert and Betsy-Ann. She remembered how often she had held them in her arms and thought: *'I wish they were mine!'*

She loved them. They loved her. Robert always ran into her arms the moment he caught sight of Aunt Ginny – his little freckled face beaming a welcome. In fact he had no time for his own mother when Gina was in the bungalow.

'He's not like that with anyone else,' Myra once told her sister. 'You've got a way with kids, Ginny. You're a natural mother. I can't think up all the games you invent to amuse them.'

Maybe adoption was the answer. Hundreds of people *did* adopt babies.

Gina dived long slim fingers into her handbag. She took out the slip of paper on which the specialist had written the names and addresses of two Adoption Societies. A little of her absolute misery evaporated as her fertile imagination began to picture one of these Societies. A room full of tiny babies. She and Charles would walk down the rows of cots, looking into each small face until they saw the child they wanted. They were so united in thought they would almost certainly decide on the same choice. Why, they'd both known at once that their cottage was 'the one'. It was the same with everything else – they liked the same people, places, food, colours, books, television programmes – and the rest. They were absolutely united in thought as well as their passionate need of each other.

The guard, passing along the corridor again, glanced into Gina's carriage. He was an astute man and noticed that the girl's expression had changed, and that there was even a smile at the corners of her mouth.

'Silly I was,' he told himself. 'Fancy thinking a lovely young woman like that would want to do away with herself. Why, she probably has everything in the world she wants, and what *I* want is my brains testing.'

To Charles it was always good to be home. He was forever telling himself that he was a lucky man. His wife – the personification of his boyhood's dreams and ideals of womanhood – and this little place which they had found by great good luck when they started to search for a home.

'Mill Stream Cottage' was one of those typical small Sussex homes built of brick and timber, with a long sloping roof, diamond-paned windows and Elizabethan chimney stack. There were only four rooms and a kitchen but it had been well modernized with the exception of the cramped little bathroom which they didn't like, but they adored everything else. The tiny garden with the flagged path sloped down towards the stream. They were more or less under the shadow of an old disused mill.

They had to walk up a long rutted lane to reach the first dwelling which was a farmhouse, then another quarter of a mile to the village of Thaxham. And Thaxham meant one tiny general stores-cum-post office, and the Wheatsheaf Inn. Otherwise it was another two and a half miles on to Hartfield and civilization.

It was the sort of artist's dream cottage that usually fetched big money, but the Mill was so much the back of beyond, that the previous owner – an artist in fact – had sold it at a moderate price to Charles – moderate for this day and age, anyhow. Besides which many people imagined that the millstream made the place damp. But Charles and Gina were young and healthy. They didn't mind a bit of damp, or woodworm in the beams – or the isolation. They had their little car and Charles' wrought-iron factory was not far from Brighton. It all fitted in nicely.

Things seemed even better when Charles' brother-in-law, Malcolm, found his modern bungalow on the outskirts of Hartfield and bought it so that the sisters were in walking distance of each other.

Malcolm was a 'commuter'. He went up to London to his job every day. He was on the Stock Exchange. He was not Charles' type but Charles didn't have to see much of old Malcolm anyhow. He brought his own friends down to Mill Stream Cottage for the odd weekend. Gina was good at entertaining and liked it and he adored showing her off, knowing that her warm beauty of which his friends were well aware, was his own.

His main ambition was to make a big thing of his factory, build on to this cottage, and raise a family. Of course by that time he would have paid off all his little debts such as the mortgage down here and his instalments on the Morris and the television and so on. Then he would be able to give Gina suitable furs and jewels to set off her glowing loveliness and they would have a foreign nurse-girl (something better than the three-times-a-week daily who came from the farmhouse just over the hill). And he would finally send the boys to Public School. (He had that rather snobbish fancy for a Public School, because he, himself, had only been to a Grammar School.) The Morris would become a secondary car, because he'd buy a Jag for his Gina, and Charles was fond of a good car. But he had not so far had any such ambitions satisfied. He had been the eldest

35

in a family of three boys, sons of a hard-working doctor in Reigate. His mother had been widowed while Charles was still quali-fying to be an engineer. Both he and his brothers had done nothing but work hard as far back as Charles could remember. But he didn't mind that. He liked a challenge. He was a young man with a forceful character. What he wanted he'd *get*. Just as he'd got his gorgeous Gina.

She had been living at that time with her parents. They had a house in Norbury where Gina's father practised as a dentist. Her family had been no better off than Charles' and that was why Gina had to work. So she and Charles had both begun the hard way. But now they were utterly blissful together in their fairytale cottage which not only had a millstream running beside it, but a walnut tree on one side of the garden, and a tulip tree on the other. Who could ask for more? Charles had not so far done any gardening in his life, but he had already bought books on the subject and was determined to have a go. He was also looking out for a chance to buy that next-door field (when he could afford it). The children they would have one day would want a tennis court. He intended to bring his sons up to play games.

Charles came into the drawing room and held out his arms.

'Hullo, my Lollo – how's things?'

She ran into his arms. He hugged her against his sheepskin-lined jacket. It felt cold against her warm hands. His lips, too, were cold as he kissed her.

'Frost tonight!' he said, glancing across the small but charming room to the brightly burning log fire. 'Gosh, Gina, it's good to be home.'

He and Gina walked arm in arm to the fire. She helped him out of his jacket, a little excited as always by the large masculine body suddenly filling the tiny room; by the tobacco-smell and the warmth of his arm against her side.

'What's cookin', good-lookin'?' he teased.

'Steak and kidney pudding!' she said. 'I thought...'

But he was no longer interested in food. His wife was soft and sweet-smelling, freshly bathed and changed as always, waiting to welcome him home. God, he would never get used to the thrill of having Gina here every night, looking like something out of one of those glossy magazines she read. She was clever about clothes. He knew she didn't have many dresses but she wore a variety of clever accessories and at night, velvet pants and an Italian embroidered sweater. She was slim enough to look fine in slacks. She liked gay colours and always seemed to look new and appetizing and exciting to him – like her red, thick, satiny hair which was brushed up high on her head – another touch of Italy.

'I oughtn't to muss up this,' Charles said, his mouth against her head. Then suddenly hard and demanding on her lips. 'Oh, darling, I do love you so much. Each time I come home it's like seeing you for the first time.'

'I know!'

She closed her eyes luxuriously, leaning on him. She understood what he meant. That quick electric spark of physical attraction was never far below the surface. It drew them together with a certainty that was almost frightening, it was so urgent and compelling.

'I ought to have a bath!' Charles whispered. His hands now caressed her back through the thin white wool of her jersey, and slid down to her waist. Suddenly he pulled her hard against him. 'Come upstairs, Gina.'

The long wait for him was forgotten as she walked up the steep oak staircase, his arm warm and exciting round her small waist. She went into the tiny bathroom and switched on the heater and then the taps. In their bedroom next door, she could hear Charles flinging off his clothes. She lit a cigarette and smoked it happily.

Presently, he came in, wrapped in his blue towelling dressing-gown and quite unselfconsciously, plunged into the hot water there in front of her. She sat watching him, a little shyly. Even after a year of marriage, she could not quite get used to the idea that his body belonged to her just as hers belonged to him. It was still only in the darkness that she could lie quietly feeling the firm muscles of his shoulders and let her hands wander exploringly over his body.

'I love you to do that!' he said often. But she couldn't be so uninhibited in the day-time. Charles teased her sometimes about this.

'I love your shyness. Somehow, it makes each time like the first time. We'll never let our love-making get matter-of-fact, will we, darling?'

It never was. Now, as Charles rubbed himself dry, she could feel her heart thudding. Her breath was coming quickly, unevenly. The tension mounted as he lifted her into his arms and carried her through to their bedroom. He was so strong – so very masculine.

Slowly, he began to pull off the sweater, neither of them cared now about her hair, and it fell around her shoulders in the way he liked it best. His gaze never left her face, his hands were gentle but impatient. At last she helped him.

'I love you. I'm crazy about my wife, Gina.'

'Yes, I know!' she whispered back. 'I'm

crazy about you, too.'

But quite suddenly, this time it was different. She was no longer close to him in her mind as their bodies moved together. Her spirit was wandering away into a new sad loneliness.

How was it possible that two people who loved as she and Charles loved – who could find such perfection and joy in shared physical passion, could not conceive a child? If they had not been so well suited; if they had loved each other less; if Charles were impatient or she, cold and unresponsive – then perhaps she might have understood their sterility. But it was all so perfect.

'Gina, darling, what's wrong?'

Always perceptive in his act of love, Charles had sensed the change in her; the withdrawal of her spirit.

She fought against herself and clung to him more fiercely, digging her hands into his arms and whispering:

'I'm all right! Darling, believe me!'

For a second, passion flared between them again – then died. Charles held her with hands that were gentle and remorseful. She was trembling.

'Sorry, dearest. I didn't realize you didn't want...'

'But I did – I do,' she broke in, 'Oh, Charles!'

Suddenly she began to cry. The tears ran

down her cheeks on to his bare shoulders. She gasped with the effort to control herself.

'Gina, dearest! Darling, my darling Lollo – what's wrong?' He tried to quieten her, to lift himself up, but she pulled him down and clung to him more tightly, as if she were afraid.

'Gina, you've got to tell me what's happened. What's wrong with you? What have *I* done wrong?'

She shook her head in fierce denial.

It was still a moment or two before she could tell him. She had meant not to give him the bad news until after he had had their evening meal. But now – suddenly the whole unhappy story began to pour from her.

'I feel so awful about it!' she ended. 'It's as if I've cheated you. I ought to have gone to a doctor and found out before we married. I'm so *sorry!* But how could I *know?*'

He stroked her hair with great tenderness. He fought against a desire to laugh. He was really relieved. He had imagined … well, he wasn't quite sure what he had imagined, but certainly not what she had just told him. But it would have been God-damned awful if she had stopped wanting him.

'It doesn't matter!' he said gently. *'It just doesn't matter, Gina.* Don't you see, dearest, that nothing matters so long as we have each other. That's the basic necessity.'

She sat up, her eyes still wet. She looked at him uncomprehendingly.

'But, Charles, you *wanted* us to have children one day. You said so. We were going to have four...' her voice broke a little. He grabbed at her hands and held them tightly.

'And now we aren't! So what? As for you feeling you've cheated me, what nonsense! I swear to you, darling, that even if I'd known about this before our marriage, I wouldn't have given it a second thought. I would have rushed you to the altar just the same. It was *you* I wanted – not the kids.'

She swallowed but frowned uneasily, grabbing for a handkerchief, blowing her nose. In a way, what he said was infinitely comforting. No doubt he meant it, too. But at the same time, she felt he *ought* to mind.

'Charles, it's wonderful of you to take it like this. It makes me feel better but it's still perfectly grim. I wanted a baby – I do want one badly. I want *your* child. Charles, since that can't happen now, we could at least adopt a baby. The specialist suggested we should. I know it couldn't be the same, but at least...'

She broke off. Charles had pulled away from her. His face had grown serious.

'I wouldn't want to do that, Gina,' he said quietly. He stood up, found a cigarette and lit it – not looking at her now.

'But *why* not?' she exclaimed. 'After all, lots of people who can't have children adopt them. You feel in time as though you really are the father and mother and, of course, the babies never know any other parents. Myra knows a family who say they feel their adopted kids are absolutely theirs.'

But Charles said quietly and firmly:

'I don't want anyone else's child if I can't have yours!'

2

After they had eaten, Gina brought up the subject of adoption again.

They were lounging lazily together on the sofa which Charles had pulled nearer to the big log fire in the inglenook. It was January and outside the night was bitterly cold. The wind had swung to the east.

'*Why* are you against the idea of adoption?' she asked Charles in a low, worried voice.

He did not answer at once. He leant forward and threw on another log, his mind at the same time admiring the wrought-iron screen which was of his own design and making. Then he said:

'I'm just not keen on the idea, darling. Don't let's talk about it any more, eh? I am really not so upset as you seem to be because we can't have kids. After all, we've only been married a year and I'm quite happy to keep you all to myself. I'd probably be wildly resentful of the time you had to spend changing nappies and mixing bottles.'

Gina was silent. Instinct warned her not to press Charles too hard but she was still not accustomed to the idea that he did not agree

44

with her on this matter. It was their first dissension. She felt unhappier than ever before. It would have been better if at least he saw her point of view...

'But I *need* a baby!' she said almost sullenly. 'There's nothing much for me to do while you're away at work. I – I get lonely.'

Charles looked at her in surprise.

'Do you? You've never said so. I thought you went to the bungalow most afternoons.'

'So I do! I help her with Robert and Betsy-Ann – but Charles, that's Myra's life, not mine. They are *her* children.'

'Well, they are your close relations, darling.'

Again she was silent. A slight feeling of resentment because Charles was being rather stupid over this matter, made her edge away from him. She sat up, leaned forward, hugged her knees with both arms, and stared into the fire.

'They aren't my children!' she said again.

Charles gave her a quick surprised look and frowned. He wished Gina would stop worrying. He liked her old gay, carefree, responsiveness. Their evenings were, as a rule, full of laughter and fun – or shared interest in a good T.V play. Tonight she refused to switch on. She wanted to talk and talk about this visit to the specialist which he wished she'd never made.

'So you're bored with me already?' he

asked lightly, but with an effort to restore the balance between them plus a shred of hurt vanity.

At once, she was in his arms, filled with remorse.

'I didn't mean that. If I could be with you all day, perhaps I wouldn't mind about the baby. But when you aren't with me, time drags, darling.'

He gave her a quick kiss on the tip of her nose. He was quite happy again with his ardent Gina in his arms. He said:

'I'll tell you what! Why not a part-time job? You could surely get one in some shop in Hartfield? – antiques or something? Go in by bus.'

'But you said you didn't want me to do a job.'

'I only meant you didn't *have* to work – that I could quite well afford to support my wife. But I imagined you'd find more than enough to do looking after the cottage and me. It's different if you're bored. I've no objection to your earning some pocket-money, my love.'

This time she did not reply. While she had been in the Norbury department store, when she first met Charles, she had been happy enough. She got on well with the other girls. Her life was busy and at times fun. But now the thought of going back to selling clothes, or even antiques which fascinated her, as alternative to raising her own and Charles' children, appalled her. How was she to make him understand?

The following afternoon at the bungalow, Myra said:

'I'm sure Charles will come round in time. After all, he is only twenty-six and I don't think many men are born with the paternal instinct. I know Malcolm wasn't particularly interested in babies until Robert was actually born. Tell you what, Gina – bring Charles round to lunch on Saturday and we'll dump Betsy-Ann on his lap. She can't fail to appeal to him – she's just the right age – all dimples and smiles and your hair and eyes.'

Gina looked at her sister gratefully.

'Oh, Myra, do you think that might work? It sounds too simple. It's deadly all this – proving so much more difficult than I thought, to make Charles understand. He seems to think my wanting a baby so badly is a reflection on himself – that he's not enough in *himself* to keep me happy. It isn't remotely that. You know me and how I dote on Charles. I suppose it's just that I'm a woman and I naturally want a child.'

'Even someone else's?' Myra asked as she deftly changed Betsy-Ann's nappy and put her back in the playpen.

Gina lifted Robert from her lap and put

him down on the floor, too. For a moment or two, the little boy struggled to get back to her, and Gina, smoothing his fair curly hair and looking down into the flushed freckled face, said:

'Yes, I could love someone else's child. If anything happened to you and Malcolm, I could bring up Robert and Betsy-Ann just as if they were mine. When a child loves you, I don't think you can fail to feel a tremendous response.'

'Well, I don't think *I* could,' Myra said. 'Perhaps that's because I've got two of my own. You can't altogether blame Charles. I don't know that Malcolm would like the idea of adoption. Somehow or other, a man's pride is involved.'

'But it isn't *his* fault we can't have our own,' Gina argued. 'It's mine.'

'M'm!' her sister agreed doubtfully. 'But somehow it just doesn't seem the same – adopting a child.'

'Well, it's going to be the same for me,' muttered Gina.

The following day, she visited her father and mother. Mr Oliver had retired now from his job as a dentist. They lived in a neat little semi-detached house still in Norbury – but smaller than the one in which Gina and Myra had been born and brought up.

Gina waited until her mother had poured out the tea and then she said:

48

'I saw a famous gynaecologist on Monday and he told me I can never have children. I – I'm thinking of adopting a baby.'

Her parents reacted at once. Her father, who was placid and a little unimaginative like Myra, said slowly:

'Best not to rush into anything, my dear. You're young yet and the doctor might be wrong.'

'But he's one of the biggest specialists on the subject in the country,' argued Gina. 'He was absolutely certain.'

'All the same, I'd wait a while,' Mr Oliver said, lighting a pipe. To Arthur – his pipe was a cure for the deepest depression.

Mrs Oliver shook her head.

'I don't think adoption is a good idea, Ginny. I knew one woman who adopted a little boy – he grew up a thief and ended in Borstal and she was a devoted mother. It broke her heart. Bad blood will out, you know.'

Gina's face grew pink with indignation.

'You can't condemn all adoptions just because one goes wrong. There was probably a good reason for this one you mention. As to your remark about *"bad blood will out"* – why should an adopted baby have bad blood? I presume you mean it *inherited* bad traits?'

'Well, yes, dear!' said Maud Oliver uneasily. 'I imagine most children available for

49

adoption are illegitimate.'

'And what's that got to do with it?' Gina asked.

Her mother was flushed with embarrassment. This was hardly the kind of talk she liked round a tea-table ... but Gina always had been an impulsive, forthright girl. A headstrong one, too. Not as placid as Myra. Yet Mrs Oliver had always loved her beautiful younger daughter best. Gina – christened Georgina after her grandmother, had charm and warmth and had endeared herself to the family from the earliest days. That ardent colouring was amazing, coming as it did in this rather colourless family – all of them blue-eyed and fair haired. But Dad was dark. He was a quarter Italian on his mother's side. She had been auburn-haired. That accounted for Gina's special type of beauty.

'A woman who has no morals is not a *good* woman!' she said at last, rather pleased with her choice of words, and smiling at Gina.

'But, Mum, you can't say that. Just because a girl has made one mistake, it doesn't mean she is *bad*.'

'But the weakness of character is there,' said her mother, stubbornly. 'No, I don't think I'd like the idea much, Ginny. I'm surprised Charles hasn't put you off the idea – he's so sensible.'

'Charles *is* against it.' The words were out

before Gina could stop them. She was furious when she saw her mother looking pleased.

'There, I knew my instinct was right. I know it must be very disappointing for you, Gina, but it's God's will and it's not right to fight The Almighty who shapes our destinies.'

'Oh, Mum, this is ridiculous!' exclaimed Gina, her cheeks burning with vexation. 'You can't write off everyone's infirmities as God's will, and say therefore one should do nothing about them. Unwanted babies in Homes need parents just as much as I, in my way, need a child. Why should we all go without, and lead incomplete lives because someone has made one mistake? I refuse to believe that that is "God's Will".'

'Well, don't shout, dear,' said Mrs Oliver soothingly. 'I'm sure if you are patient, you will end up with a baby of your own. As your father just said, doctors are often wrong, even the best of them. Why, I know someone who waited twelve years before their first baby came. The couple had given up hope. Then after the first, she had twins, so...'

'But I don't want to wait twelve years!' Gina broke in. 'I want a baby *now*.'

She caught the train back to Hartfield deeply disturbed. There seemed to be no one on her side – first Charles, then Myra, now her parents had lined up against her. Only Mr Naughton-Irving had seemed to understand and approve her urge for motherhood.

During the ensuing weeks, this urge became an obsession with Gina. She gave up going to see her sister and the children, because she found herself unable to bear the sight of another woman's fulfilment. Often, when Charles was asleep, she cried silently and uselessly. She lost weight and grew pale and pensive. Charles tried to 'jolly' her out of her depression. It depressed him. She was such a changed being. He knew what was on her mind but he refused to be drawn into any more discussions about adoption. They had been to that lunch at the bungalow, and on the way home, Gina with a sly look at her husband, had said:

'Don't you think Betsy-Ann is a *poppet*? I wish she was ours, don't you, Charles?'

He had given her a strange, sideways glance in return and announced:

'Frankly, babies don't appeal to me all that much. She's a pretty little thing and I like her because she's like you, but … look, darling, I think I know what you were trying to do today. Well – don't do it again, sweetie. It won't work. I just don't want anyone else's child. Now do let's forget about it, shall we?'

She was appalled that he could forget so

easily. But she went on remembering and suffering torments of frustration. In an effort to please Charles, she actually applied for a part-time job in an antique shop in Hartfield and they took her on. She started to work there three days a week. At any other time, the work would have interested her for she loved beautiful things and the elderly man who ran the shop was a very considerate and pleasant person. But she could never lose herself for long, and as she dusted the ornaments or books, her mind would wing back to the thought of the baby she so desperately wanted.

'You must try to snap out of it!' her own sister told her one afternoon when Gina visited her and dissolved into tears. 'I know you pretty well, Ginny, and you're a great one for wanting what you can't have. It was the same with poor Mark – because he was always there, figuratively speaking, on his knees to you, you never gave him a serious thought. Then Charles came along. Remember you told me you were sure he was married because of that signet ring he wore on his left hand? That started you. You went crazy about Charles, and Mark faded into the background.'

Gina blew her nose and sniffed indignantly.

'It isn't true. It was only on our first date I thought he was married. I loved Charles at first sight – it had nothing to do with my not being able to have what I wanted.'

'You're letting this baby business become an obsession, anyway,' Myra answered with her father's cool obstinacy. 'When you come over to me you can't talk about anything else. You must spend half your life reading books on the subject. It can become a bore, darling.'

It was true and Gina knew it. She had already obtained three books from the local county library. Each one had added to her desire to adopt a child. The thought, ever foremost in her mind, was how to persuade Charles to let her have her way. She must. She *must*.

'Charles,' she said a month later. 'Would you at least agree to do one thing for me? Come with me to one of the Adoption Societies. Hear what they've got to say? It wouldn't mean you had to commit yourself in any way – but at least it might make you realize that what I want is a normal, every-day affair. Do you know that there are thousands and thousands of adoptions every year in this country alone. Look at this pamphlet–'

Charles' mouth tightened.

'Statistics don't alter my *feelings*, Gina. I don't want someone else's child. I don't think I could ever get to love it and quite apart from my own feelings, it would hardly be fair to the child itself to come into a home where only one of the parents wanted it.'

'But if you saw it – if we just had a baby here in the house for a bit – on trial. You know, Charles, a baby can come on trial for three months. I've found out all about it. I rang up one of the Adoption Societies. Once you've selected a baby, you fetch it home, then if you aren't still sure after three months, you can keep the baby for another six months, to make absolutely sure.'

The expression on Charles' lean brown face did not change. His eyes were less warm and understanding than she had ever seen them. They were almost cold. Gina's heart sank.

'I hate having to say "no" to you, darling,' he said. 'You must know I'd much prefer to be able to give you anything you want.'

Her cheeks flushed a bright pink. She ran to him and grasped his hands.

'Then please, *please*, Charles, let me have this one thing. Let me at least have a baby here on trial. I swear if at the end of the period you don't want it, I'll let it go back to the Society. Please, darling!'

His face softened. With that unusual colour on her creamy face and those large appealing eyes, it was hard to resist her. But he had made up his mind. Over matters such as this, it was best to be quite firm from the start. He didn't want an adopted child. A son or daughter of his own – yes, that might have been fine. But babies as such held little appeal for him. He felt it would be quite unfair to Gina – and the child – to have one 'on trial' (as if it were a damned puppy, he thought irritably). It would undoubtedly have to be returned and then Gina would be even more disappointed and upset.

He tried to explain his feelings. Gina was usually so quick to catch his meaning, to follow his line of thought. Now he was annoyed by what he felt to be sheer stubbornness on her part when she refused to accept his arguments.

'The trial idea is exactly made for people like us,' she persisted. 'The baby would be too young to be upset by the change and we wouldn't have had it long enough to mind so terribly if it went back. Charles, I give you my solemn promise I won't ask you to keep it if you don't want it in the end. But how can you *know* you wouldn't like it without trying?'

'Well, how can you know you *would* want it for good?' Charles argued heatedly. 'If you can be so sure, so can I.'

That night – the first in their married lives, they lay far apart on separate sides of the bed. There was no goodnight kiss – no comfort for either of them in the other's warmth and nearness.

Charles fell asleep first. Listening to his quiet regular breathing, Gina felt her resentment and depression grow with each passing minute. It wasn't fair! *It wasn't fair!* Charles refused to accept that she was a real woman. He was selfish – wanting her only as his lover, denying the mother-urge in her. He looked at the problem only from his own point of view – never hers.

It was no longer just the thought of her childlessness which was making her so unhappy. It was the rift between Charles and herself. She could hardly believe that two people who had been so close could become strangers because of the first real problem in their lives.

'But I won't give in to him – I won't!' she told herself fiercely. 'If necessary, I'll go ahead on my own. I'll go to the Adoption Society alone.'

She did not yet know that both parents had to want a baby before any Society would allow them to take a child – even on trial.

She slept deeply at last, exhausted by her emotions and by the subconscious dislike of planning anything of which Charles would disapprove. In her sleep she moved closer to him and when they awoke, they were once more side by side.

3

Gina watched Mark as he threaded his rather bulky frame through the crowded lunch tables towards her.

'Dear old Mark!' she thought with affection. She had not seen him since her marriage to Charles and in a way, she had missed his friendship.

Mark was not the kind of boy one felt romantic about. He had a rather snub nose and freckles and a shock of untidy fair hair. His best feature was his eyes – large, darkish blue, fringed with unexpectedly dark lashes that would have pleased any girl. Those eyes had always been full of rather shy adoration. Gina used to notice it but it meant nothing except that it was flattering – she just was not in love with Mark.

Now, suddenly, she found herself valuing Mark's steadfast devotion as she had never done before. The last time she had seen him, on the day before her wedding, she recalled something he had said to her.

'If ever you want me for anything, Gina, no matter what it is, I'll be waiting. I'll never stop loving you. Promise me you'll call on me if I can ever be of help.'

She had thanked him but at the time been sure she would never need Mark's help. How could she need anyone, once married to Charles? Now, only eighteen months later she did need that help and quite badly.

She had telephoned Mark at his office in Hanover Square where he worked as a junior architect. She had asked him to meet her for lunch at a small Soho restaurant – one he used to take her to on occasions in the past.

'I know it's very last minute notice,' she apologized. 'But I need your advice, Mark.'

So here he was, sitting opposite her, looking exactly the same as she remembered him, unruly hair, freckles, college tie – and all. The overgrown schoolboy. But very much a man.

For a moment, they were both a little shy. Then Mark with the old warm admiration in his gaze, looked at the charming figure in the dark grey coat with the fur collar and the cossack hat on the beautiful red head, and said:

'You look a treat, but, gosh, you've got thin. Come on, let's order our food and then you can tell me what's up.'

Gina made him choose for her. She was not in the least hungry. Now that the moment had come, she was suddenly afraid of what she had to say to Mark. While he decided on the special minestrone and pasta she used to enjoy, she sat thinking about this morning. She had been to one of the Adoption Societies. There she had learned that before anything at all could be done about adopting a baby, she must make an appointment for an interview. Both her husband and herself must be present at this. Then, and only then, if she and Charles were found suitable, would they be put on the waiting list for a child.

This had shaken Gina. In the first place, she knew well that Charles would refuse to attend such an interview. In the second, if there was a long waiting list for babies, she could not afford to sit back and wait for Charles to change his point of view. She had been equally upset to learn that there was no row of babies in cots from which to choose. Apparently the Society picked out an infant they thought suitable and asked you if you were willing to take it.

Gina had gone into a shop in Oxford Street, ordered a coffee, and wondered what to do. It all looked hopeless. Without Charles' co-operation, there was nothing she *could* do. It seemed to her again that life was terribly unfair. Yet at the same time, she could understand the Society's point of view. A baby needed two parents to love it if it were to be happy.

But Charles would – in time he *would!* Gina kept assuring herself miserably. If she could only take the infant home and let him get used to the idea of having it around – become familiar with its little ways, he could not fail to love it. He was a warm-hearted, loving person, really. There was nothing cold or restrained about Charles, and he used to talk about that tennis court for *his* son.

'Well, Gina, tell me the problem,' said Mark, 'and have a glass of sherry.'

'He's like an elder brother!' she thought. Yet that was not quite true. Subconsciously, she was beginning to count on Mark's blind adoration – his loyalty to her – something one was unlikely to get from a *brother* – to back her up in her predicament.

'You've got to help me, Mark,' she said urgently. 'You've just *got* to. There isn't anyone else I know who'll do it.'

He looked into the grey velvety eyes – as lured by them as ever. He listened while she told him first about the specialist, and then her husband's reaction to the question of adoption. As she went on to recount the details of her visit this morning to the Adoption Society, Mark looked more uneasy – especially when she told him what she had in mind.

'It's only for an hour, Mark!' She was openly pleading now. 'You've only got to *pretend* to be my husband for one hour. Once we are put on the waiting list, I'll have plenty of time to talk Charles round. He'll never know you impersonated him. Mark, please!'

Perhaps Mark Rendell knew already that he would never do as she wished, although he had rarely been able to deny Gina anything. Once or twice her sister Myra had told him not to be such a doormat for Gina.

'She'll never marry you if you go on behaving like her slave.'

Now he knew to his cost Myra had been right and he had lost Gina – to Charles. But he could not alter his nature. He never really expected Gina to fall in love with a dull old stick like himself. And because he didn't hope for the impossible, he had been able to enjoy her friendship without too much heartache. His love for her was quite selfless.

He believed that he was unattractive to women – too conventional, too ordinary. He also had a strong sense of right and wrong. The thought of impersonating Gina's husband was so impossible he wondered how Gina could have brought herself to ask this of him.

Gina sensed his thoughts. She leaned nearer to him.

'Mark, it isn't in order to do anything wrong. It's only to get me – Charles and me – on the waiting list. Don't you see, it's more or less only a formality. You won't have to sign anything – you just sit there and answer questions as if you were Charles.'

'Gina, I can't. I'm sorry, but it's quite out of the question.'

He saw the quick downward droop of her mouth and the light go out of her eyes and he said quietly:

'It's not the right way to go about this, Gina. I understand how important this is to you – you're a woman and naturally, you want a child. But you can't cheat over something like this. It's too serious. Your husband would take it pretty badly if he found out.'

'I don't *want* to do it this way!' Gina broke in, nearly crying. 'It's Charles' fault – he just doesn't seem to realize what it means to me.'

Mark cleared his throat. It hurt him to see her so upset and yet he had to make her see sense. She'd always been impulsive – she obviously hadn't stopped to think of the consequences.

'Give him time, Gina. He'll come round once he knows the way you feel.'

It was on the tip of her tongue to cry out:

'He does know!' But a sudden awareness of loyalty to her husband prevented her from speaking. She felt utterly deflated. It had probably been a mad idea to expect Mark to agree. Unfair, too, to have asked him to do something she knew in her heart to be wrong.

'How would you react – if you were

Charles?' she asked.

Mark looked uncomfortable. He needed time to consider his reply. As things were, he couldn't imagine himself refusing Gina anything in the world she wanted. But then he wasn't Charles. Maybe the man cared about children – enough to mind if they were his own flesh and blood. He, himself, was too blindly in love with the girl beside him to bother his head about their children. If adopting babies would make Gina contented, that's all he would concern himself about – or at least, so he thought now. Maybe if he'd been married to her some time, he'd see the wider issues.

He ignored the question and said gently:

'He'll come round in time – I'm sure he will. Try and be patient, Gina. Surely you can wait a little longer.'

She took the train home and went straight up to her bedroom to change into slacks and jersey. Mrs Banks, the daily had lit the fire in the inglenook so downstairs it was warm. But in her bedroom Gina shivered and hurriedly drew the curtains across the darkening sky.

Before going down to the tiny kitchen to make herself a cup of tea, she went into the spare room. She and Charles called it that but in her mind Gina thought of it as 'the nursery'. At the moment the walls were papered in a plain cream. She stood in the doorway looking round with speculative eyes. She would redecorate it, nether pink nor blue, but a pale yellow, perhaps, so that it wouldn't matter if the baby turned out to be a boy or a girl. Last week, in the market, she had noticed some pretty Walt Disney curtaining – quite cheap but absolutely right for a child's room. There would be other things she would need, too – a karri-cot, a baby's bath, and later a playpen…

She realized suddenly that her imagination had led her beyond the realms of possibility. For the time being, there could be no 'nursery', no cot…

She sat down on the spare room bed and burst into tears.

She cried for five minutes but it afforded her no relief. She dried her eyes, feeling slightly ashamed of herself. Nowadays she did nothing but cry, it seemed. She wondered suddenly how so much joy could disappear so suddenly from her marriage. Months ago, she and Charles hadn't had a care in the world. No two people could have been closer, in spirit as well as being physically close. It was hardly believable that this misunderstanding over her need to have a baby could have been so effectual in separating them. They were almost strangers.

Gina's mouth tightened in swift resolution. Nothing, no one must come between herself and Charles. Whatever happened, she must remember that her marriage was more important than anything else.

But even as she went downstairs to the comparative warmth and cheerfulness of the drawing room with its blazing fire, she was doubting her own resolution. Charles just wasn't enough – she *needed* a child and that need was as great as her need for a complete marriage; indeed, marriage had become incomplete without a child.

When Charles came home, she was particularly gay and talkative. Watching her smiling, animated face, he could not guess that she was trying to hide from him the fears she had for their marriage. Subconsciously, she felt that if Charles saw nothing wrong between them, there would be less chance of a barrier. She had reached the point of being afraid to let him know her fears, or even to face up to them herself.

Charles was most relieved.

Poor darling! She had been so depressed lately – letting the baby business get on her mind. It was wonderful to think that she was getting over it at last, and was once more her gay, charming self.

He did not like to remember the uneasy tension that had laid its heavy hand on the household these last few weeks. They had spoken to each other in monosyllables. Silences that were somehow unavoidable, fell at frequent intervals. Gina had looked tired and unhappy and he hated to think, no matter how necessary, that he was the cause. If he could have given in to her with a quiet conscience, he would have done so. But he did not want a child – someone else's child – to make a third in their small household. It would have been quite different if it had been his and Gina's own baby, a little human being created by them – the fruit of their shared passion.

He loved Gina deeply – too much to be weak when ultimately only strength and resistance could solve their problems. He looked upon her obsessive desire to adopt a baby as a purely temporary reaction after learning she could never have one of her own. That fact had come as an unpleasant shock. But in time she'd accept it. Besides, he insisted that there was still a possibility that the gynaecologist was wrong. Then how would they feel, saddled with an adopted extra child they did not want.

He could admit now – when Gina sat glowing and vivacious at the table opposite him – that he had a few qualms about his decision. She'd seemed so dead set on the adoption idea. He knew, too, that she resented what she thought his lack of understanding and that this resentment had put a hateful barrier up between them and affected even their love-making. His physical need of her was a continuous hunger. He had tried in a hundred little ways to woo her back.

He frowned uneasily, remembering the several occasions when she had given in to him and he had taken her in a kind of rough desperation that held none of the joy or pleasure of their earlier relationships. Afterwards he had lain silently beside her, wanting to apologize, and not very pleased with himself. But pride prevented him from being the first to break the silence between them.

Now, tonight, he believed that Gina was all right and her old self again. When, in a little while, they went up to bed, he knew instinctively that she would not turn away from him.

He did not realize that Gina's passionate responses that night were born partly out of fear.

Was anything – even a child – worth the risk of losing Charles' love and trust? She was no longer so sure. Lying in his arms she felt an internal need to cement the bonds that held them close.

She clung to him, kissing him again and again until they no longer seemed to be two separate beings. Instead, they were one – the very core of their world, crying out with unintelligible words, uttering their joy in life and in their love.

Only later, when Charles lay sleeping, his

dark head on her breast, did tears begin to fall. Passion had afforded an escape – but only a temporary one. Tomorrow he would be off to work again and she would be alone with her hopeless craving for a child.

4

Charles was even later home than usual on the following night. He barely glanced at Gina's pale face or seemed to notice her red-rimmed eyes. He gave her a quick kiss then went over to the cupboard to pour himself a drink. He didn't often do this and she knew at once that he was worried.

She wondered suddenly if he had found out about her lunch with Mark. So far there had been no real opportunity to mention it. Besides she knew she could not tell him the real reason why she had got in touch with Mark. Charles would certainly want to know why they were meeting again.

But it wasn't that... During the evening meal Charles informed her that his foreman had collapsed at work and been taken to hospital in Brighton. He had called there after work and seen one of the doctors. The news was grim – the man had a serious heart condition and certainly could not return to work.

'And old Frost was more than just a foreman – his were the practical brains behind the business. You remember, Gina, that I took him over when I bought up the firm.

All the other men are young and inexperienced – we haven't had time to give even the most promising of 'em the kind of training they needed in order to walk into Frost's shoes. I'm afraid it'll probably mean a serious step down in production. You and I may have to do some economizing for a bit.'

'Oh, is that all!' Gina burst out and quickly tried not to show her relief, by adding:

'Of course, I'm terribly sorry about Mr Frost, but it only means a temporary upset, doesn't it? You'll find someone else.'

Charles' face looked tired. He lit a cigarette.

'I hope so. That kind of labour is scarce, Gina. We may find the going tough, you know. It's probably just as well you've started work again. And what a blessing I didn't give in to that silly notion of yours to adopt a baby. That's one thing we *certainly* couldn't afford.'

Gina's face puckered. Her hands tightened. Charles, slumped on the sofa, looked up at her properly for the first time that evening. For weeks now she had been her normal self. They had seemed as close as they used to be in the first months of their marriage. He was convinced she'd forgotten all about the adoption. Now, looking at her taut face, he wasn't so sure.

'You weren't still hoping I'd change my

mind, were you, darling?' he asked anxiously and held out a hand.

She ignored it and said flatly:

'Yes, I was.'

Charles' face darkened. His mouth set in a hard, stubborn line.

'Well, it's out of the question, so the sooner you forget about it the better.'

She opened her mouth to plead with him but the words would not come. She said coldly:

'Are all husbands as selfish as you, Charles?'

He stared at her incredulously.

'Selfish? Me? Good God, Gina, *you* talk about selfishness! Here I am in the middle of a business crisis and you start a quarrel over a hypothetical child.'

Gina's eyes were flashing. The angry colour stung her cheeks.

'Your business, not mine! You'll sacrifice anything, everyone, toward your ambition. You don't care about mine, do you? Who's the complete egotist?'

A faint glimmer of understanding went through him. His voice was more gentle, patient, as he explained:

'Look, darling, my business is for both of us. I admit I want it to be a success – but only for us as a pair. I want to be able to give you a decent life and home, reasonable comforts. I can't do so without money.'

'You only want for me the things you want for yourself!' Gina flared, beyond control now. 'Money would buy everything *you* think worth while, but it won't help me to get what I need so badly. You can't *buy* a baby, Charles. No… You can keep your money. Personally, I'd be far happier if we had none at all. At least then there would be some real *reason* for your refusal to let me adopt a child.'

'You're talking like a fool!' Charles said flatly. 'You know as well as I do that you who love beautiful surroundings, would loathe an existence in a furnished bedsit, for instance. Don't cheat, Gina. When we got engaged we used to talk about our future and plan it mutually. We seemed to agree about it then.'

'I didn't realize that I wasn't going to be able to have a baby.'

'You didn't make such an issue about a family then!' Charles flung at her. 'It's become an obsession and a damned un-healthy one at that. For heaven's sake pull yourself together. Go and see Dr Whatshis-name. Get him to give you some tranquil-lizers or something. I can't put up with much more of this.'

She stared at him incredulously. Then she ran out of the room. He calmed down a little. He had an idea Gina might be upstairs crying on her bed, but for the moment he felt little desire to go up and comfort her.

She was, he told himself, behaving unreasonably – no matter how much she wanted this adoption. If anyone was being selfish, it was Gina. If she'd had any real love for him, she would have been concerned over his business crisis and been sympathetic, and all out to make him feel less worried. He'd had a packet today – without *this*.

Resentment fought with his natural kindliness. But at last he could no longer bear the thought of Gina upstairs, miserable and alone. He sighed and went in search of her.

She was there, as he expected, on the big double bed, face-downward – crying wretchedly. The sight of her stirred his tenderness.

'Look, darling,' he began, and put a hand gently on her shoulder. Her face was buried in the pillow so he could not see her expression. 'Let's not fight any more, sweetheart. I'm sorry if I seemed a bit – well, hard. But it's been a grim day and I'm damned worried and fagged out. Sit up, darling, and tell me I'm forgiven – let's be friends again.'

She shook her head violently. She couldn't give in. She knew that it would not help either of them to quarrel now. She didn't *want* to quarrel with him, but childishly, she saw no reason why she should be prepared to see his point of view when he was unwilling to look at hers.

She remained silent, her shoulder stiff and

unresponsive beneath his hand. They remained in silence for a few more moments. Then Charles said:

'Very well! If this is the way you want it...'

'It isn't, it isn't...' She wanted to shout at him, but the words choked her and she twitched away from his hand again. A moment later, she heard the bedroom door close.

She beat the pillows with clenched fists, her body trembling with frustration. She felt utterly defeated but this time, she could not cry. With her, anger and sorrow had gone beyond tears.

5

A week later, Mark came down to the cottage to see Gina. She was pleased to see him. Since her quarrel with Charles, which had not been made up – the days had seemed even more boring and lonely for her than usual. There were no longer even the evenings, the nights with Charles, to look forward to. They lived now like strangers. She cooked the meals and served them and talked in a quick, stilted little voice about the few domestic happenings of the day. Charles, equally stilted and ill at ease, mentioned what was going on at the factory. Nothing more. No kisses, no fun, no laughter. At night they lay at opposite sides of the bed, terribly aware of one another but each unwilling to make the first move towards a reconciliation.

Gina found Mark's unexpected visit a welcome distraction. He found the cottage and surrounding country fascinating. He roamed over the old mill. He tried to be gay and casual. Then he stopped putting on an act. He was acutely sensitive to Gina's mood and aware of her unhappiness. He sat opposite her by the log fire and said gently:

'Things aren't any better then?'

She shook her head.

Mark touched her hand with his.

'I was afraid not,' he said. 'I'm terribly sorry I couldn't help the way you wanted me to.'

Gina sighed.

'That's okay, Mark. I understood. You were probably quite right, anyway.'

He looked at her heavily shadowed eyes and unhappy mouth.

'Poor dear – all last week I was racking my brains trying to think of a way to help. Finally – and I hope you don't think I've been betraying your confidence, Gina ... I had a chat with a doctor pal of mine.'

She looked up quickly, sudden interest brightening her expression.

'Oh, Mark, what did he say? Did *he* know of a baby I might adopt without Charles being involved?'

Mark shook his head.

'No, it's not that. But he did suggest it might make the waiting easier if you went to work in a crèche – at least, that's what he called it. I gathered it's a kind of home for children under five whose parents can't look after them.'

The hope vanished from Gina's heart – and eyes. She said quietly:

'Don't *you* understand either, Mark? It isn't just that I want a child to look after – I want one I can call my own. I want mother-hood.'

Mark nodded.

'I know. But this chap, Burrows, said the children at the crèche are quite often placed with foster parents and later on adopted. He thought, perhaps, if your husband was given a chance to get *used* to a child…'

Gina suddenly understood. She jumped up and threw her arms around Mark, her cheeks bright pink.

'Oh, Mark, I see. What a terrific idea. It's just the kind of arrangement I was hoping to make. I *know* Charles only needs time … he loves kids. If we had one in the house he'd grow attached to it! It might be the answer.'

She was like a little girl, dancing round the room excitedly; now making plans; rushing to the telephone to ring her own doctor and ask where the nearest crèche was to be found.

The man watched her with mixed feelings. Part of his heart would belong to Gina always. Yet at a moment like this, he realized more than before that his lovely volatile girl with her swift passions, and deep, even primitive emotions, could never belong to him. It wasn't just that Charles had snatched her from his grasp but that she had never really been within his reach. She needed a husband, a lover, with a personality as strong and vivid as her own.

78

She went on talking vivaciously:

'Oh, Mark! If you can only guess how much better I feel already. It's just as though you'd raised a curtain and shown me the way out. Now at least I can believe there is hope again. I can't think how I failed to hit on this plan myself. It's so simple. Night after night I've lain awake, wondering how it could be done. Let's celebrate – let's have a drink – oh, I wish we had some champagne in the cottage.'

She was like champagne herself – he thought – sparkling and beautiful, full of effervescence, a changed being.

They spent the rest of his visit to her discussing the plan and embroidering on it. He let her talk and make plans without a thought for himself or his own feelings for Gina until it was time for him to leave her again.

When Charles returned from work he did not need to be told that something had happened to restore Gina to all her former beauty and gaiety of spirit. She looked radiant. She had changed into a scarlet velvet après-ski suit which she had bought to wear at the cottage on winter evenings. It seemed to turn her into a glowing flame, he thought, and stared at her.

'Oh, Charles, darling!'

She actually flung her arms round him and kissed him. He kissed her back, a little bewildered and nervous, half afraid that the other depressed inarticulate Gina of the last few months would reappear.

'Something nice happened?' he asked, and walked over to the fire and spread cold hands to the warmth.

Gina joined him and linked her arm through his.

'Yes!' she said. 'But I've not come into a fortune if that's what you might think!'

He glanced sideways at her. He wasn't sure if there was a hidden barb in her words, knowing that Gina had recently taken to despising worldly goods because money couldn't buy her what she in particular wanted.

'Come on then, tell!' he smiled, feeling indulgent and tender toward her again.

She was suddenly shy, afraid he wouldn't understand.

'Whatever it is, I'm glad it's made you so happy!' he added. 'Tell me what's happened, darling.'

She began to formulate Mark's plan for him, the words rushing out. She couldn't, of course, tell him everything; not that she secretly hoped to find a foster child which later she might adopt. But she said that she had decided to work in a crèche and knew all about it and how she had already discovered one where they were short of helpers. On the bus route, too, so she could get there.

'Don't you see, Charles. I can do the kind of work I'll enjoy and you won't have to bother about driving me there if you want to stay late at the office. I'm going for an interview tomorrow and Dr Williams says there's no doubt I'll get a job.'

Charles looked faintly bewildered. Even as he began to congratulate her he felt somewhat out of his depth. Gina's excitement seemed to him to be quite out of proportion to the facts. He could understand that working among babies might bring some satisfaction to a certain type of woman but not Gina, surely! Why, she was the glamour-girl type and not only glamorous but far too intelligent to spend her time spooning food into grubby little mouths all day. Somehow it didn't quite add up.

'Isn't it marvellous? I'm so thrilled!' she kept saying.

He sat down on the velvet cushioned sofa beside her and put an arm tentatively round her shoulders. It had been a long time since they had had any kind of physical contact. He wasn't sure if she would draw away from him. But she only smiled up at him and snuggled closer. His heart began to beat with a heady intoxication. He could feel the warm softness of her through the smooth coat and knew that he wanted her desperately. His desire was so overwhelming that he had to fight with himself to go slowly with her. He was afraid that he might lose control and just make mad love to her, with or without her consent.

He heard her quickened breathing; saw the quick rise and fall of her breasts and knew that she, too, felt the same sudden desire.

He swung her round and with rough, eager hands began to pull off the scarlet velvet jacket. She did not try to stop him, but raised her own fingers to help him.

He whispered:

'Oh, my God, I want you, Gina!'

Later, she lay in his arms, her face glowing in the firelight. There was a half smile on her lips. Utterly content, she remembered the sheer wonder and excitement of their love-making.

'You know, darling,' she whispered. 'I can't understand how it can go on being so different. Doing the same things with the same person, one would imagine there would be no surprises left for married couples – but with us...'

She broke off, sensuously closing her eyes.

He kissed her mouth and held his hand against her breast.

'I know! Perhaps it is because we almost lost each other.'

'Not *really!* I didn't really stop loving you, deep down.'

'Nor I you. You are happy now, aren't you, sweetheart? I can't bear it when you're miserable.'

'I'm very, very happy, Charles.'

They lay in silent contentment until he said:

'What gave you the idea of working in this children's home, Gina?'

'Idea? Oh, Mark suggested it. Funny I never thought of it for myself.'

'Mark.'

'Yes, he came down to lunch. I was going to tell you...'

She broke off as Charles sat up and began to pull on his clothes. She watched him, a little warily, puzzled by his changed expression.

'Darling?' She sat up and leant on one elbow, watching him dress. 'Darling, you didn't mind Mark coming down?'

'You invited him, I suppose?'

'No, I didn't, as a matter of fact. He just turned up. But even if I had, I don't see why you should mind. You aren't jealous of him, Charles?'

He refused to look at her or to answer her question. In fact, he had always been a little jealous of Mark; or perhaps he had been jealous of the years Mark had known Gina before he, her husband, ever met her. Sometimes he had wondered whether Gina's assurance that she had never cared that way for Mark and that it had been a completely one-sided affair, were really true. But now suddenly he felt thoroughly disgruntled. For weeks he'd tried to think of some way to bring a smile to Gina's face and failed. It was Mark who had come to see her and waved the magic wand that had so completely transformed her. It infuriated Charles.

'Oh, Charles dearest, you old idiot!' Gina began to button up her velvet coat. 'You can't possibly be jealous of poor old Mark. Why, he's on your side. When I...'

She broke off, suddenly aware of what she was about to reveal. So far, Charles knew nothing of her request to Mark to go with her to the Adoption Society and pretend that he was her husband. He must never know either. She was already ashamed of even having suggested such a crazy thing.

'Well, go on!' Charles' voice was hard now, as well as curious.

'Oh, nothing! Let's forget about Mark, shall we? Let's just be happy. It's been so good, feeling happy again.'

'And we can thank your precious Mark for your good mood, I take it.'

She swung round to stare at him reproachfully.

'Charles!' She couldn't bear the thought of quarrelling with him again. Besides, it was so ridiculous...

'Look, darling, Mark just gave me the idea

… that's all there is to it. Now please, let's forget him.'

Charles walked away from her. He opened the cupboard and poured himself out a drink. He stood there, his back to her. His voice was cool and unfriendly again.

'It isn't quite so simple. For him to come here and make suggestions means you've discussed our private life with him. I suppose you've also told him we couldn't have children of our own and that I was such a selfish brute I wouldn't agree to adopting one. No doubt he consoled you, is all on your side and sympathizes with you for marrying a man who has failed all along the line … even in his business. No doubt you both sat wishing you'd married each other.'

Gina gasped, her face a dull red. She walked across to her husband and grabbing his arms furiously swung him round to face her.

'I ought to slap your face for that!' she cried. 'How you could say such filthy things just after … after … oh…' Her voice broke and she burst into tears.

Charles threw up a hand in mock dismay.

'Off we go *again*. Seems I can't do anything right these days. Now I've made you cry again. Damn it all, Gina, when are you going to grow up. You're a spoiled, hysterical child.'

He knew he was being nasty and unfair

but he couldn't stop himself.

She stormed back at him.

'Maybe you're right and I should have married Mark! At least he would understand me – and what's more he'd have done something about it when he knew I couldn't have the one thing in the world I needed.'

'So now we're hearing the truth!' Charles said scathingly. 'Well, if you want a divorce, I won't stand in your way.'

She put a hand to her lips and looked at him with wet, unbelieving eyes.

'Of course I don't want a divorce. You must be out of your mind.'

'I'm not the one who's been complaining. You're the person who is so miserable. *You're* the one who wasn't satisfied with me. Remember? The one who found life with me such a bore and had to have a child as well. Oh, no, Gina, you aren't going to be allowed to shove the blame on me.'

'I'm not trying to shove the blame on anyone!'

'Don't shout!'

'You're shouting at me!'

They stood looking at each other helplessly, furiously. Then anger simmered down in Gina. She felt desperately afraid of the formidable wall that Charles was building between them.

'Oh, Charles, please don't let's quarrel. I was so happy and you were so marvellous just now. Can't we go on being that way.'

He took the hands she held out. But it wasn't the same.

They ate their meal, exchanging only studied, unnatural conversation. Later, they watched television, and stayed up until the end, each as reluctant as the other to face the intimacy of the bed they shared, now that they had become strangers – even enemies again.

Gina finally went upstairs before Charles. When, after a carefully calculated interval, he joined her, Gina was already asleep. He slipped into the bed beside her, taking care not to wake her.

The barrier was back, strong, higher and less penetrable than it had been before.

Charles was worried. Gina was so totally absorbed in her work that he felt he had completely lost her. For the first two weeks, she refused to talk about her work but after careful probing, he discovered that her whole life, while he was at work, now revolved round a two-year-old girl whom they called Linda.

He wasn't prepared to admit it even to himself, but he was consumed with jealousy of this child. Whenever Gina mentioned Linda her whole face lit up and her eyes glowed in a way they had used to do only for him. She seemed to concentrate all her thoughts, her passionate protective affections on the wretched little girl. Linda's case history was unpleasant. She was recovering from a brutal assault by her own father. He was 'doing time', Gina informed Charles. The mother had eight other children and was weak, helpless and utterly under the influence of her husband.

In order to keep some link of conversation between them, Charles encouraged Gina to talk although he resented her interest in this new job, and in the child in particular. But unless they talked of her, it seemed they must sit in stony silence. Gina's face would become withdrawn. She would seem remote and sad, lost in thoughts that he could not share. It was terrible to him – as though their marriage was disintegrating under his very eyes.

For a little while Gina's health improved. She began to look fitter, as well as happier. But as the weeks went by she became quiet again and seemed under the weather both physically and mentally. There was a new little line developing between her brows, a line of worry, of pain that hurt Charles curiously.

'What is bothering you?' he asked her suddenly one evening.

They had been watching the Perry Mason series and as it ended, Gina gave a long, deep sigh.

'You're not, by any chance, getting bored with your work at the crèche, are you?'

Gina shook her head vehemently. The look she shot at him seemed to accuse him yet again of failing to understand her.

He said with a touch of bitterness:

'Well, if you won't tell me what it is that worries you, how can I help?'

Gina got up and walked restlessly to the window. She pulled back the curtains and stared into the dark of the garden. She was fighting with the temptation to tell Charles the truth. And the truth was, she wanted Linda. During these last two months, the little two-year-old girl had wound her thin little fingers round Gina's heart in such a way that Gina knew she could never be free again from the fierce protective love that had grown in her.

When she had first come in contact with the child, Linda had seemed just a pathetic little bundle of fear. But gradually she had come to trust and rely upon Gina. Now Gina was the only woman working at the crèche who could persuade the child to eat, settle her down to sleep, make her take her medicine.

Yesterday Matron had said:

'We've got to try to make her a little less dependent upon you, Mrs Martin. You see, if you had to be away for any reason, I think it would have a bad effect on Linda. It's not, after all, as though you were really her mother, although it's obvious you've replaced the mother in her affections. It's a pity but one should not allow any such fixation while these poor children live in a Home like ours. I hope and believe Linda's mother will agree to her eventually being sent to foster parents. That, at least, would give the child some security.'

'You mean, the mother isn't going to take her home again?'

'The Children's Officer is dead against it. She thinks Linda's father suffers from some kind of psychological hatred of the child and that when he comes out of prison, he will harm her again. The mother is a hopelessly weak character. She agrees that Linda may be in danger but can't bring herself to accept the idea of parting with her.'

Gina's heart began to race. She said quietly:

'If her mother does agree to it eventually, could I be her foster mother?'

The matron looked at the beautiful girl with some surprise. It had astonished her since Mrs Martin joined the helpers, that she seemed so passionately interested in this type of work.

'Why, I had no idea you would contemplate any such thing, Mrs Martin. Of course, it would mean we should lose your services here.' The older woman smiled. 'And I've often wondered now how we managed before you came – you've been simply splendid with Linda.'

'I love the work, especially looking after Linda. I can understand now how nurses feel in hospitals when they've pulled a child through a serious illness; I can also understand how necessary it is for them to try to be impersonal. I'm afraid I've let myself become deeply attached to little Linda and if it would be permitted, I can think of nothing that would make me happier than to take her home and devote my life to her.'

Matron raised her brows but smiled.

'You realize the impermanence of fostering? It is not the same as legal adoption. Any time the mother would have the right to demand that the child be returned to her.'

Gina lent forward, her beautiful eyes blazing.

'But if it came to the point, Matron, would the courts allow her to do that? Linda's mother has admitted the father may turn on her again.'

'I know! Let's hope the wretched woman decides for herself that it would be best to part with the child. I daresay if she knew the child was coming to you ... she'd be influenced by that.'

Gina tried to make her voice sound casual, although a sudden excitement seized her.

'Maybe I could take Linda home one

evening – just so that my husband can get to know her. There'd be no harm in that, would there, Matron?'

That was what had been said between them.

Now Gina looked across the room at her husband and with the same excitement and hope, she said:

'Will you be home early tomorrow evening, Charles?'

'I could be if it's something special.'

His voice sounded warmer, more interested. Gina took heart.

'Well, I'm bringing Linda back for the night. I thought after all you've heard about her, you might be interested to see the child.'

Charles did his best to conceal his disappointment. He had hoped Gina had decided after all these months to do some entertaining, for even if it was only Myra and Malcolm, it would have shown her reawakened interest in the world outside that damned crèche, he thought. He could not look pleased or interested now. But he tried not to damp her enthusiasm.

'Oh, well, I'll try and be home by five. I'd quite like to take a look at this kid who interests you so much.'

Gina's natural impulse was to fling herself into his arms and kiss him; to show her gratitude and relief in a physically demonstrative way. But a sixth sense warned her not to let Charles know how much his acceptance of Linda meant to her. If he suspected at this stage that the meeting was the means to an end, he might put his foot down in that firm, stubborn way she was beginning to dread. It was so final.

While Charles stayed to watch another television programme, Gina slipped away up to the spare room. Hurriedly, almost guiltily, she began to prepare for Linda's coming. There was no cot but she made up the spare bed and pushed over the small chest of drawers against the side so that Linda would not fall out. Then she filled a hot water bottle to air the mattress.

When this was done she hurried back to her own room and searched in one of the cupboards for a fluffy white rabbit. She had bought it some weeks ago for Betsy-Ann's next birthday but now she would give it to Linda – her first present here in this house although she had already bought the child several small gifts.

Gina's eyes shone with secret happiness as she went back downstairs to make tea. Charles seemed to be immersed in the play. She seated herself quietly beside him. For the first time in months, she felt content, at peace. Tomorrow night, little Linda would be asleep upstairs and she never doubted that Charles would be attracted to the child and gradually grow so fond of her he would not want to part with her ever.

No one, she told herself confidently, could fail to love Linda. She was so tiny – like a little Dresden figurine. Perhaps she wasn't exactly beautiful, her little face was too thin, her body too angular. She was by no means a cuddlesome, adorable type of child. The shock of her father's assault had left her with a nervous twitch of the shoulders – a look of fear in her big eyes – a sad suspicious expression which she lost only occasionally. Then she would give a quick appealing smile. Yes, thought Gina, appealing was the word to describe Linda. Her very fragility and those huge sorrowful eyes could not fail to arouse a protective instinct in a man like Charles.

Without fully understanding the cause, Charles sensed the new excitement in Gina. When they went upstairs together he linked his arm in hers and pressed it close against him; her soft fragrant body sending the old wild thrill of desire through him.

'Tired?' he asked softly.

She shook her head.

'No! I don't think I could go to sleep quickly. I might read for a bit.'

But he had no intention of letting her read. When he lay beside her, he took the book from her and began to caress her. Gina turned to him, her face relaxed. She wound her arms round his neck, drawing him closer. Life, once again, was proving a wonderful and happy affair. Charles still loved and wanted her, must want her to be happy, too. Otherwise he would never have agreed so readily to allow Linda to come here. It was all going far better than she had hoped. After all, he could have refused… She felt deeply grateful to him. She reached up and kissed him.

'Darling!' Her voice was in itself a caress.

'Gina, my Gina – my adorable darling!'

He was in love with his wife. He forgot the irritation he had felt earlier; forgot Linda's existence. At moments like this nothing mattered but that his beautiful wife should belong to him, completely. He wanted her like this always, his alone, with no other thought in the world but their love.

Only later did he remember that tomorrow night they would no longer be alone. He tried to recall some of the things Gina had said about the child. There had been some sordid event in the past but he couldn't remember the details. He wasn't sufficiently curious to bother too much about it – after all, it was not as if it could touch their own lives. This was no baby waiting for adoption, trying to compete with him for Gina's love and affections. And since there was no threat to his happiness, he could afford to be tolerant about her having the child to stay.

In fact, in the morning when Gina woke, he'd surprise her by telling her that she could have the child for a whole week if it made her happy. It wasn't really *so* much of a price to pay in return for the shining happiness in her eyes and for nights like this when she seemed so tender, so loving and grateful to him.

He put his arm across the narrow waist. He could feel the gentle rise and fall of her breast as she slept. He could see her lips moving as if in a kiss – as if she was dreaming of him.

Fortunately for his peace of mind, he could not guess that it was a child's name, and not his that formed on those moist red lips, which he touched in a final goodnight kiss.

6

Gina's nerves were at breaking point. This morning Matron had said that Linda's mother had finally made up her mind to let the child go to foster parents.

'It would be as a preliminary to adoption,' she had said. 'How would you and Mr Martin feel about it?'

Gina was filled with new wild hope.

'I'd adore to keep her with me. You know that!' Gina said, with deep feeling.

And Matron, looking at her, thought, 'This girl is sincere – a real mother at heart – most unusual person.'

But that same evening, Charles delayed his homecoming until the child was asleep, and before Gina could open the subject of Linda's future, he said:

'You've been looking after that child nearly two weeks now, Gina. Isn't it time she went back to the Home? After all, it's hardly fair to the kid to let her get too used to our household.'

Gina looked at him in silence. All the various speeches she had planned seemed to fade away. She did not know how to begin to tell Charles that if he forced Linda away from her now, she could never, never be happy again. But instinct told her to keep a threatening hysterical outburst under control. Turning her face away she spoke quietly:

'Linda hasn't been a nuisance, has she, Charles? I mean, you've hardly noticed her around.'

Charles stiffened. He'd been steeling himself to bring up the subject for a week. Now that he'd started, he intended to go through with it. It wasn't that the child had been a bore. The poor little devil was almost too quiet to be true and certainly scared to death of *him*. Gina had explained the reason for Linda's fear of men but although Charles had felt equally disgusted by the story of the assault of a man on his own baby daughter, it did not change Charles' views about having the child permanently hanging around his home.

The fact that Gina worshipped the little girl was all too obvious although she did her best not to make too much fuss of Linda in front of him. The last thing he wanted was tears and recriminations when the child had to go back to the Home. It stood to reason that the fonder she became of Linda, the worse she'd feel.

It never occurred to him to allow Linda to stay. As he was away all day and the child nearly always asleep when he got home at night, he had seen very little of her. There had been only the one weekend when they had taken her over to Myra's for tea and then he'd managed to sneak off to the garden with Malcolm, leaving the two sisters to gossip by themselves while they minded the children. No, he had no special feeling, unless it were pity for the little girl. The real reason why he wanted her out of the way was because he foresaw trouble with Gina...

'She's been as good as gold, Charles. And going to bed tonight, she kept asking when you'd be home. I think she's getting quite fond of you and trusts you now.'

Charles downed a glass of beer and lit his pipe.

'That's just the point. She's getting far too used to being with both of us. It's unfair to keep her here. Frankly, I'm surprised the authorities have allowed it.'

Gina bit her lip. She wasn't sure if Charles was being deliberately obtuse about things or if the idea of keeping Linda permanently had really never occurred to him. She said hesitantly:

'Unless you really don't want her around, darling, she doesn't *have* to go back. We ... we could become foster parents and then ... if you grew as fond of her as I am ... we could adopt her.'

Charles' face flared an angry red as the import of Gina's words hit him. His eyes closed and unclosed – as though he had to struggle to keep calm. Finally he said in a low angry voice:

'So that's behind all this. Now I see your game. And I was fool enough to be taken in. You really are a little cheat, Gina. All this time you've been trying to bluff me while you carried out a carefully pre-conceived plan!'

Gina's face was colourless. She was prepared for Charles' objection but not for that bitter, merciless condemnation.

'I suppose that delightful boy friend of yours, Mark, put you up to it,' he went on with sarcasm. "Let the child worm its way into the home and then Charles won't have the heart to turn it out". Well, I can tell you this much, Gina – *Linda's not staying. I'm not going to let you be a foster mother and I'm not going to adopt her.* Do you understand?'

'But, Charles, I love her!' The words were wrung from Gina.

He walked across the room and gripped her by the arms. His fingers hurt her. His angry, bitter eyes hurt her even more.

'Love? Do you know the meaning of the word? You say you love me yet you go behind my back and play this rotten trick on me.'

'It isn't a rotten trick!' she cried, her lips trembling. 'I was only trying to give you time to feel as I do about Linda. I thought you'd grow to love her, too. I thought you'd see how much she meant to me and let her stay – for both our sakes. *You* talk of love, Charles, but where is your love for me? Is it so much to ask? You know how badly I want a child. Well – now I've found Linda, I'm not going to let her go. If you force me to it, I'll leave *you*. But I'm not giving *her* up.'

She broke off, appalled by her own words. Anger and a deep hurt had led her to make the threat she wasn't even sure she would carry out.

Charles was as white as she was now. For a moment, he stared at her as if trying to fathom the extent of her threat. Then he said very quietly but clearly:

'You will take Linda back to the Home before I return tomorrow. That's final. No more arguments. You know my views. I shall not alter them.'

Gina lay on the bed, her head throbbing with pain. She could not even cry. It was as though her once-adored husband had dealt her a physical blow – as well as a mental one. She ached everywhere. She was hot and shivery at the same time. Her throat was dry. But when she had tried to get up to go to the bathroom for a glass of water she felt so giddy she fell back on the bed, eyes closed, every limb feeling as though it was weighted with lead.

She thought dully, 'I've had a cold and cough for weeks; I haven't been feeling at all well!'

But she had said nothing to Charles. She had been so afraid any complaint about her health would trigger off a command from him to get rid of Linda. It was the one thing she had dreaded, and now it had happened.

Laying pride aside, she had called down to Charles, but he was still out at the pub where he had stormed off, putting an end to their angry discussion. She was quite alone in the house with only little Linda asleep in the room next door.

She lost count of time and lay in a stupor, her mind filled with torturing thoughts of losing first Linda, then Charles. She could not seem to follow through to a conclusion any one train of thought. Each one became confused and took on the quality of a nightmare.

Sometime later, she was aware that Charles was in the room. She made a supreme effort, called him over to the bed and asked him to give her a drink. A little later she heard Linda crying. And then as she struggled to go to the child, Charles said:

'It's all right, darling. I'll go!'

By morning Gina was very ill. She had developed pleurisy. Charles sent for Dr Williams, the local M.D. After an examination he talked of sending her to hospital. But

Gina, although only semi-conscious, heard what they were saying and became nearly hysterical.

'No … no … no! I won't leave Linda!'

Her voice seemed to echo through the large, burning cavern of her throbbing head.

Charles sat down by her side and took one of her hot hands in his cool fingers. All his latent tenderness and love for her had revived. He was full of remorse because he had not noticed that she was ill and had been so brutal and unsympathetic. He was aghast at his own harsh egotism.

He was desperate with worry. Most of the night Gina had tossed and turned, wet with perspiration, in a high fever. By the time the doctor returned in the morning, she was delirious. She cried constantly for Linda and occasionally, in her more conscious moments, called for Charles and begged him to listen to her incoherent appeals.

He telephoned Myra to come round. Myra had recently acquired a Danish girl with whom she was able to leave the children.

In the drawing room, he had a hurried consultation with his sister-in-law and the doctor.

'The sooner Linda is sent back to the Home the better!' Charles announced. 'The nurse Gina needs can sleep in Linda's room.'

'But Charles,' Myra argued. 'Gina'll go out of her mind if you send Linda back. You can't do that to Gina now – not whilst she is ill. Besides, I thought you had agreed to become Linda's foster parents prior to adopting her. Gina said last week...' She broke off and looked from Charles to the doctor in an embarrassed silence. 'I'm sorry,' she said at last. 'Seems Gina let hopes and facts get a bit muddled – or else I got the wrong end of the stick. Incidentally, where is the child?'

They found Linda sitting on the landing outside Gina's bedroom, quietly rocking her doll in her arms. Myra picked her up and carried her downstairs. She looked at Charles reproachfully.

'Has she had breakfast?'

He shook his head.

'Then I'll get her some.'

He followed her into the kitchen.

'Look!' Myra said. 'I've got an idea. I'll lend my Danish girl, Ilse, to you. She's had nursing training although she isn't qualified. Would that be all right, Doctor? Then she can keep an eye on Linda at the same time. I know we can lend you a camp bed which can go in the spare room. Ilse won't mind sharing with Linda, I'm sure.'

Dr Williams did not seem very happy about the lack of professional care for his patient but at the same time, he doubted very much if he'd get a bed for Gina in an overcrowded hospital at such short notice. The main thing was to start her on antibiotics and if she didn't respond other arrangements would have to be made. He gave Myra a prescription to have made up at the chemists on her way home and left the cottage with her, promising to return later in the day.

Charles saw them off and then wandered back into the kitchen feeling helpless and extremely worried. Myra and the doctor had taken control of his household and the child, apparently, was to stay.

He glanced at the highchair and found Linda's large thoughtful eyes regarding him enigmatically. The plastic mug of milk was untouched. He wondered uneasily how much the child understood of what was going on; if her worried expression were really one of concern for Gina. The poor little thing looked scared to death, but then that was hardly to be wondered at with all the strange comings and goings. He'd be glad when Myra got back with the Danish girl and he need not feel responsible for Linda.

He held the mug with awkward gentleness to the child's mouth and obediently she took a few sips; then she raised her arms to be lifted out of the chair. He put her down on the floor, surprised at her ethereal weightlessness. He'd never actually held her before. He was shocked to find her so thin and light.

It occurred to him that she might not have had sufficient breakfast but before he could find a loaf of bread, she had run out of the room. He heard her soft footsteps on the stairs and then the landing.

He hurried after her. He must prevent her from going into Gina's room. Gina was on no account to be disturbed. But Linda had once more seated herself cross-legged outside the door, like a forlorn puppy. She gently rocked her doll and hummed a tune which Charles vaguely recognized. He had heard Gina singing it to her at bedtime.

He stepped past the child into his wife's room. Gina was sleeping fitfully, her face very flushed and her body restless beneath the clean sheets Myra had put on the bed. He sat for a few moments holding her hand, longing for her to open her eyes and talk to him. But she was obviously either exhausted or under sedation.

Suddenly, he remembered their quarrel and how he had walked out of the house in a temper and left her here ill and alone. He almost shook her to wake her so that he could tell her how sorry he was. Then he remembered the cause of the quarrel and his anger with himself turned once more on the child. Linda was the cause of the trouble between them. The moment Gina was better, the child *must go.* He had foreseen just this crisis when Gina had first asked him to adopt a baby. He'd *known* he could never love a strange child and that it would give rise to trouble between them. Gina couldn't really have meant her threat to leave him rather than Linda. She'd been semi-delirious at the time only he hadn't realized then she was ill.

No doubt part of the trouble lay in the fact that she had over-tired herself at that damned nursery. She had quite enough to do looking after him and the cottage without spending eight or more hours a day minding a lot of kids. He ought never to have allowed her to take the job.

When Myra came back with the Danish girl, Ilse, Charles was still sitting by the bed blaming his own weakness for Gina's illness; and the child was still sitting, silent and rocking herself gently to and fro, outside the bedroom door.

7

The Child Care Officer was a grey-haired, middle-aged woman in her fifties. She had spent the last twenty years of her life dealing with people and although the questions she put now to the man sitting opposite her seemed casual enough to Charles, they were nevertheless guaranteed to extract the revealing kind of answers she required.

Charles felt awkward and embarrassed. He had never expected to become personally involved with Gina's work at the Home and but for her illness, he would have refused to see this Mrs Cooper in order to discuss Linda's welfare. He had already tried to explain that he did not wish to be responsible for the child in any way, but that he was prepared for her to remain in his home in the care of the Danish girl until his wife recovered.

'You see, she has a kind of obsession about Linda. When we first found out we couldn't have children of our own she wanted to adopt a baby. Then she went to work in this children's nursery or whatever you call it, and unknown to me practically took over the child, Linda. I never realized quite how much it had come to mean to her until…'

He paused, looking away from the steady blue eyes regarding him thoughtfully.

'Yes, Mr Martin? Until…?'

'Well, until just before my wife fell ill. We … we had a row because I refused to agree to become a foster parent to Linda and she threatened to leave me if I wouldn't let her keep her. Of course, Gina was hysterical at the time…'

He was not very convinced of this fact himself, but he hoped Mrs Cooper believed him. After a minute or two, she said:

'You realize that my job is to see that Linda's future is a secure and happy one? I have to put her first. She can't go on living with you and your wife unless you are *both* willing to fill in an application form to become her foster parents.'

Charles leant forward on his chair, his face anxious.

'I quite understand your point of view. Frankly, I don't want the child here. But I must agree to keep Linda until Gina is well. You see, she's sort of got the child on her mind. The doctor thinks if Linda goes away now, it will have serious consequences for Gina. She's just not in a fit state to see that it's far best for everyone for the child to go back to the Home at once.'

Mrs Cooper nodded.

'If you are quite, quite sure *you* won't

change your mind, then you are absolutely right, Mr Martin.'

Charles looked pleased.

'Well, I'm glad *you* understand, Mrs Cooper. Frankly, you are the first person who does see my point of view. Gina's sister … oh, well, no need to go into details. You see, Mrs Cooper, I'm very much in love with my wife, however trite that may sound to you, I don't really want to share her affections with anyone. I don't see why she should need anyone else but me. It's not as if I neglect her. I've nothing at all against Linda personally – she's a pathetic little thing really, and one doesn't like to think of her without people to love her. But it's not my job – *or Gina's* – and that's all there is to it.'

Mrs Cooper gave a half smile which she carefully hid from Charles.

'I take it then that this objection to keeping Linda isn't due to any personal prejudice. You'd feel this way about any child? Your own, had you been able to have one?'

Charles shrugged.

'Well, about one of our own, I suppose things might have been different. I don't know. Quite frankly, I don't feel any particular paternal urges.'

'Few men of your age do!' was Mrs Cooper's comment. 'But it is a very natural thing for a young woman to have the maternal urge, Mr Martin, and I'm afraid you are not going to find it easy to rid your wife of hers. She's a very feminine little person and one with a great capacity for love. You have your work to give added interest and satisfaction to your life. Mrs Martin needs a child just as much as you need a job to absorb your vitality and brain.'

Charles looked down at his hands and then directly into the blue eyes of the woman in front of him.

'You're suggesting that I'm being purely selfish? That I ought to give in to Gina over this?'

'Certainly not, Mr Martin. It would be quite wrong for you to pretend an affection for Linda. The child would sense the truth however kind you were to her and because of this, we could never agree to you becoming a foster parent. You must realize that she has already lived through one tragedy – living with a father who neither loved nor wanted her. We certainly wouldn't allow her to suffer that kind of rejection again.'

Charles stood up and walked across the room, thoughtfully fingering some books, then an ashtray and a box of matches without really noticing them.

'Can't you make Gina understand that?' he asked at length.

'I think she already does!'

'Then she has agreed to let Linda go?'

Mrs Cooper shook her head.

'I'm afraid not. She truly loves the child, Mr Martin. She says if Linda has to go back to the Home, she'll go with her. Of course, I could recommend to Matron that she doesn't re-employ your wife in order to safeguard your marriage, but somehow I don't think this would solve anything, would it? I think your wife is in such a state of mind that she is capable of trying to run away somewhere with the child.'

Charles swung round, his face white, his mouth open with surprise.

'You really mean she'd leave me and *kidnap* this child?'

'I think such thoughts may have passed through her mind. But you must keep calm, Mr Martin. Your wife is in a very unstable highly emotional state. That is apt to be the case when a woman is denied the natural outlet for her maternal instincts. And, of course, her state of health at the moment is only aggravating the position. You must go gently with her – just try to see her point of view, if you can.'

'And Linda?'

'I'll take the child back with me. I think it may be best in the long run.'

Charles looked uneasy.

'Gina will go out of her mind if she finds Linda has gone. And the child … well it's pathetic, really, but she haunts Gina's bedroom door. Whenever she's missing, we find her sitting up there. I … she's very attached to my wife.'

Mrs Cooper nodded.

'Yes. It is partly Linda's *need* of Gina that has brought about the fierce protective love your wife has for the child.' She tried to explain to Charles. 'Linda will find it very difficult to settle down again in the Home. Your sister-in-law did suggest that she and Mr Rendell might offer her a home so that Gina could see Linda occasionally, but I'm not too happy about the idea. I don't know how you feel about it, Mr Martin? You might object to the time your wife spent at your sister-in-law's home?'

Charles fought a silent battle with his conscience. The fact was, he would object – strongly. He'd resent, just as he always had, every bit of love Gina gave the child. On the other hand, he was afraid of what Gina might do if Linda were removed altogether from her life. Suppose her love for him turned to hatred and in her bitterness and resentment she actually left him?

He was appalled by such a prospect. His lovely red-haired Gina, who used to laugh so gaily and be so happy and warm and passionate in his arms.

'I don't really see that the decision lies with me,' he prevaricated. 'It's up to my sister-in-law really, isn't it? I'm surprised Myra offered to have Linda and even more

113

surprised that Malcolm has agreed. But that's their business...'

Mrs Cooper stood up.

'Then that may be the answer to the immediate problem. Anyway, I'll talk it over with Matron and Linda's mother and we'll see what can be arranged. Meanwhile, I wish Mrs Martin a quick recovery although I understand from the doctor it will be some weeks before she is up and about again.'

It was nearly a month before Gina was up and about again. She was still far from strong but Myra was wonderfully kind and drove over every morning to fetch her home to spend the day with Linda at the bungalow.

It was almost the end of May and the early spring made it possible for them to spend most of the day in the garden watching the children play together. Linda was still quiet, reserved, and only really laughed aloud when Gina was there. She was never far from Gina's deckchair, keeping her always in sight even when she was playing with Betsy-Ann. She was obedient enough with Myra and Ilse but never without that odd, unchildlike reserve.

Today it was Wednesday, Mark's half day off work. He and Ilse were at the bottom of the garden playing hide-and-seek with the children. For once, Linda had left Gina's side to join in the fun.

Hearing the laughter, the two sisters looked at one another and smiled. Myra said:

'Mark is a dear. You know, I think he's a little in love with our pretty blonde. He spent all last weekend here. You didn't know that, did you?'

Gina nodded.

'I did! Linda told me this morning. She seems really fond of Mark. He's the only man I've ever seen her trust. I wish...'

She fell suddenly silent and Myra, looking at Gina's thin pale face, saw the sadness there and knew that Gina was putting Charles in Mark's place. In a way, Myra could see Charles' point of view. Linda wasn't his child and if he couldn't 'take to her', it wasn't his fault. But she understood, too, Gina's bitterness. Charles had never even *tried* to like Linda. From the very beginning, he had set his heart against her just as from the start, Gina had set her heart on keeping her.

It was awful to Myra to see the slow disintegration of a marriage which had started with such promise. Not, of course, that either Gina or Charles admitted to any breakdown of their love for one another. Charles had been positively devoted all the time Gina had lain ill, getting away from work early in order to sit and read to her; bringing her armfuls of expensive flowers; showering her with every sign of love. Yet withal, he had been unable to give her what she had, and even now, most wanted.

Talking it over at night with Malcolm, Myra had asked her husband if he thought they would eventually come to a parting of the ways.

'After all, there's always old Mark in the background. He adores Gina and he told me himself he would have let her have Linda. Maybe that's how it will all work out.'

But now that no longer seemed a possible solution. Gina would never fall in love with Mark and it looked as if Mark was going to 'desert' his first love for the young, attractive Danish girl, Ilse. Myra was glad that Gina showed no sign of minding the new romance, but at the same time, she would have been pleased to see some kind of emotion, if only pique, enliven her sister's face. For weeks now Gina had been far too quiet, too uncomplaining, completely apathetic.

Suddenly the two grown-up figures at the end of the garden detached themselves from the little group of children and came walking hand in hand towards the sisters. As they drew closer, it was possible to see the shining happiness in their faces.

Still holding Ilse's hand tightly in his own, Mark said shyly:

'I've just asked Ilse to marry me and she has said "yes"! I can hardly believe my good fortune.'

Myra jumped up and hugged them both impulsively.

'How marvellous. I'm so glad for you both – though I won't pretend I'm all that surprised. I guessed something like this was in the wind. We must celebrate – we'll have a party this evening. Malcolm can go and buy a bottle of bubbly.'

Mark looked from Myra's plump maternal face to Gina's white thin one. The smile had left his eyes and he looked ill at ease, almost embarrassed as he said:

'Aren't you going to congratulate me, Gina?'

At once Gina forced a smile and stood up to embrace Ilse.

'Be good to him, Ilse,' she said softly as she kissed the girl's cheek. 'Mark's a wonderful person.'

Ilse beamed back happily.

'Indeed yes, I will. I very much love him. I try to make him so happy. I give him many children, yes? I t'ink he is so fond of the young ones.'

There was an instant of awkward silence, the reason for which Ilse was happily ignorant. Myra, though fond of her, had never confided in Ilse her sister's personal problems and the girl knew nothing of Gina's desperate desire for children or even that Mark had once been very much in love with her and had wanted to marry her.

Ilse went on chattering.

'We have first the three sons and then the three daughters,' she said. 'This is a nice size of family, no?'

Mark turned to her quickly and laid a hand on her arm.

'Don't let's plan too far ahead,' he said gently. 'We'll have to buy a house or rent one – find somewhere to live before we start thinking about a family. Perhaps you could help Ilse do some house-hunting,' he said to Gina. 'She doesn't know enough about our country yet to be aware of the possible pit-falls.'

'Yes, of course I'll help,' Gina said. 'It'll give me something to do.'

A little later, Mark and Ilse went off for a walk and Myra looked at Gina anxiously.

'Darling, you aren't upset, are you? About Mark and Ilse, I mean?'

Gina shook her head.

'You should know me better than that, Myra. I'm pleased for Mark and I think Ilse is a very lucky girl. He'll make a wonderful husband … a wonderful father.'

Myra's face fell.

'Oh, Gina, my dear, you sounded so bitter. You mustn't blame Charles. He can't help lacking that paternal streak. Can't it be enough that he loves you?'

Gina's mouth twisted in sudden pain.

'If it were true, then yes! But how can you

expect me to believe that he loves me? True love, real love, is unselfish. Charles won't let himself see that his refusal to let me adopt a child is killing my love for him. *He* doesn't want a child and that's all he thinks about.'

'Gina, that isn't true. He's quite justified in not adopting a child if he knows he couldn't be a good father to it...'

'You think so? That's just Charles' excuse for not doing something he doesn't want to do. He wants me all to himself ... not all the time, of course – but when he feels like a nice little break from work. I'm a toy, a plaything to pick up and put down again when he's tired of it or has more important things to do.'

Myra looked aghast.

'This isn't what you really feel, Gina. It can't be. When you were so ill Charles was frantic with worry. He adores you and you know it.'

'I'm glad you still believe that,' Gina said quietly. 'I don't. I think loving is giving. Do you really think *I* could refuse *him* something he wanted as badly as he knows I want a child? Of course I couldn't. He knows deep down what it means to me but he just isn't going to give in to me.'

Myra was silent. In a way, she could understand Gina's bitterness. In the weeks she had had little Linda staying with her she and Malcolm had grown extremely fond of the child. The little girl was slowly becoming emotionally detached from Gina and was putting Myra and her family in Gina's place. Even Malcolm, the quiet sensible un-emotional type, had said vaguely the other evening:

'I suppose we could give Linda a per-manent home with us if Charles and Gina don't want her back. I wouldn't want her to go back to that Home. A child needs a family and she gets on very well with ours.'

Yes, Malcolm could be persuaded to adopt Linda if Myra herself wanted the child and Myra had seriously considered the possi-bility. She would have pursued the conver-sation but for the fact that she was still hoping for Linda's sake that Charles might eventually relent. She realized that he was far less likely to do this if he knew the little girl already had a happy home in the offing.

As if following her train of thought, Gina said quietly:

'Charles will never agree to taking Linda back. He's hoping you will adopt her so he can salve his conscience the easy way. I know she'll never be mine now.'

'Oh, Gina, don't say that. Charles might change, given time. You mustn't give up hope. Linda can certainly stay here with us meanwhile – we all love her. And you know you can come and see her as often as you want.'

Gina gave a tremulous smile.

'Yes, I know. And don't think I'm unappreciative of what you are doing for Linda – and trying to do for me. But it isn't going to work. And since that is the case, it's really better that I don't see too much of the child. I know she's perfectly happy with you. A week ago, she wouldn't have left my side. Look at her now, playing with Betsy-Ann and not giving me a thought! That's as it should be, though of course, it hurts. But I wouldn't want it otherwise. I had not the right to make her so dependent on me – or to be so dependent on her.'

'You won't stop coming to see her, Gina?'

'No, of course not. But I won't come quite so often. Anyway, I won't have time, will I, if I'm to help Ilse house-hunt? That will keep me busy for a while.'

Myra relaxed. Gina's attitude was a surprisingly sensible one – unemotional and logical. It was wonderful, really, that Mark and Ilse had decided to become engaged and so provide Gina with a new interest to occupy her thoughts. She had become far too morbid and quiet and it would do her good to go up to London with Ilse and think about something else other than herself.

'That sounds like Malcolm's car,' she said contentedly. 'I'll ask him to run down to the off licence and get a bottle of champagne. Charles should be here by the time he gets back and we'll have a celebration party.'

She hurried away to intercept her husband, leaving Gina alone. Therefore she did not see the look of bitter unhappiness in her sister's eyes; nor see the nervous twitching of her hands as they clenched tightly in her lap. Least of all did she realize that for Gina the promised party was to celebrate the loss of her dearest friend, Mark; the loss of her love for her husband, Charles, and the loss of all hope that Linda might one day become her own child.

8

Charles looked at his wife's face and said anxiously:

'You're tired out. Have you been in London again all day? Do you have to wear yourself out like this?'

Gina remained staring into her coffee-cup, her face expressionless.

'I can't find a suitable house for them!' she replied after a pause.

Charles shifted in his chair. He was quite unsure of himself with Gina these days. She never raised her voice or showed any emotion and he never knew what she was thinking – whether she was annoyed, unhappy, resigned. He simply could not get through to her. For the last month, she had been up to London every day house-hunting for Mark and Ilse. At first it had seemed to him an excellent idea – at last a means of occupying herself while he was at work; and above all, a harmless enough method of forgetting the whole unfortunate Linda episode. He had been glad that Gina practically never went to her sister's now to see Linda; happy when Gina told him that she thought Myra would end up adopting the child. It seemed then that his stand had been vindicated; that once she had accepted as final his refusal to adopt a child, she would settle down and find other ways of filling in her time.

Now he was no longer quite so sure. Gina was now as much obsessed with house-hunting as he had been with Linda. Every single day of the week she disappeared on the 9.15 and seldom arrived home before six at night. It was hardly surprising that she pleaded exhaustion when he wanted to make love to her and certainly true enough that she looked worn out. She was thinner than ever and the shadows beneath her eyes had deepened perceptibly.

Thinking about her last night as he lay sleepless at her side, wanting her and yet not daring to touch her, he resolved to have a talk with her. Surely Gina could see for herself that there must be moderation in all things. It wasn't as if Mark and Ilse were in a hurry to get married. Ilse had agreed to finish her year with Myra before her wedding to Mark, so there was more than enough time to find a place to live without Gina having to walk London for them every day of the week.

Gently he put the fact to her. Gina's face gave no sign of her feelings. After a moment's silence which now seemed to follow all his attempts at conversation, she repeated:

'I can't find anywhere suitable!'

It was almost, Charles thought, as if she

were bringing herself back out of a dream-world of her own to talk to him. Her replies made sense but only just. He stayed patient with her.

'Look, darling, you admit there is no hurry. Why not go up two or three times a week, if you feel you must? Personally, I think you've done more than enough looking already. Mark agrees with me. He said last weekend that he was sure he and Ilse would find a place without all this effort on your part.'

Now he had Gina's full attention. She was staring at him from those large eyes in which there seemed to be an expression almost of fear. Her voice, too, had risen a tone.

'But I want to go. I like going to London. It gives me something to do. Please don't try and stop me – it's all I have to do.'

'Calm down, sweetheart!' Charles said quickly. 'I'm not trying to stop you doing anything you want. It's just that it does seem a little unreasonable – five days a week, six hours a day house-hunting for someone else. You're not terribly strong and you are wearing yourself to a shadow. It doesn't make sense!'

Gina frowned.

'No – no, I suppose it doesn't!' she agreed.

Charles leant forward eagerly.

'There, you've admitted it yourself, darling. Now to please me, don't go up to-morrow – make it every alternate day, if you must. What about it?'

'But I *want* to go up to London.'

Charles' patience deserted him. Gina was talking like a chid. Surely she could see how unfair it was to him to come home to a wife too exhausted even to make conversation – let alone make love.

'Look, Gina, this can't go on. I've tried to make you see that your behaviour is absurd. I'm not a Victorian husband who would forbid his wife to do something of which he did not approve but if you persist in behaving like a child, I'll be forced to treat you like one for your own sake. You'll be ill again if you go on like this.'

Gina's eyes which had looked startled when he first raised his voice, were now expressionless again. She said softly:

'You can't stop me going!'

Charles swore softly.

'For pity's sake, Gina, stop talking like an idiot. I've just said I can't stop you going and I wouldn't even try. I'm trying to make you see for yourself how stupid it all is. Why do you have to be so extreme about everything? Why can't you settle down like other wives and be normal? Do you realize that we're becoming like strangers? You never talk to me, let alone kiss me when I come home. Oh, you answer when I speak to you but I'll swear half the time you aren't really listening to what I'm saying. You're getting more and more morose and less and less easy to understand. What kind of a married life is it we lead? What have I done to deserve this – this indifference? Don't you love me any more? Is Mark's and Ilse's blasted house more important than our marriage?'

'What did you say?'

Charles gasped. He had been close to shouting in his impotent exasperation. Gina could not fail to have heard him – had she been listening.

'That's a classic example of what I was trying to say to you – you don't *care* any more. That's the root of the trouble.'

'But I do care. I care terribly!'

There was such sincerity in Gina's voice that Charles was momentarily mollified. He went over to her and put an arm round her shoulders.

'Do you really, Gina? At times it has seemed to me as if we've grown terribly far apart. I love you, you know. Very much. Too much to let you wear yourself out this way. Will you do as I ask and stay home tomorrow? I tell you what, I'll phone the office and say I'm not coming in to work. We'll go off somewhere for the day together. You'd like that, wouldn't you?'

Gina nodded.

'I could go to London the next day, couldn't I?'

Charles withdrew his arm and shrugged.

'Yes, of course, if you feel you *have* to, but I can't see why. Still, we won't argue about that. What shall we do tomorrow, darling?'

'I don't mind – whatever you want!'

Charles' annoyance gave way to fresh uneasiness. There was no spitefulness in Gina's tone – only her words hurt because they showed a complete lack of enthusiasm for the day he envisaged for them. He wanted it to be a special day, a happy, friendly day when they would laugh and be gay and enjoy life together. It was so long since he had heard Gina's laugh, seen her uncomplicated beautiful smile; so long since she had shown any kind of eagerness to have him near her; of wanting him to kiss her, hold her hand. One perfect day together could achieve so much if all went well. They would come home, close mentally and physically and go up to bed together...

His thoughts halted as he remembered his visit to Dr Williams a few weeks ago. He would never have thought of going to a doctor to discuss his marital relationship with his wife a while ago. It showed how seriously his marriage to Gina had gone wrong. But he was a normal healthy husband and he found the physical segregation difficult to accept or to tolerate.

'She doesn't seem to want love-making any more!' he had complained.

'Be patient and gentle and don't force

yourself on her,' Dr Williams had coun-
selled. 'She was pretty ill, you know – nerves
can play havoc with the body. If she isn't
feeling fit, she won't react in the normal
way. As soon as she gets physically fit, you'll
be back to normal.'

But Gina wasn't giving herself a chance to
get better – wearing herself out in London
day after day. If anything she was thinner
and paler than ever and none of Dr
Williams' vitamins seemed to be having the
slightest effect.

'I think we'll take a run down to the sea. If
it's a decent day, we might take a picnic on
the Downs. We could go for a long ramble
the way we used to when we were engaged,
remember?'

There was the barest nod of Gina's head.

'Look!' Charles said kindly. 'I'll wash up
supper – there isn't much. You cut along to
bed and get a really good night's sleep –
then you'll be fresh for tomorrow. Yes?'

'Thank you,' Gina said quietly. 'I would
like to go up now.'

Charles washed up the dishes in better
spirits. If not enthusiastic Gina was showing
some co-operation. He hoped tomorrow
would be fine. He hurried through to the
sitting room to switch on the T.V forecast
but picked up a boxing match instead on the
other programme. It was nearly eleven when
he heard the news and decided to follow

Gina up to bed.

Because he did not want to disturb her, he undressed in the dark and it was not until he was getting into bed that he realized Gina was not there. For a moment, he stared at her empty place in numbed confusion. This gave way at once to a nameless fear. She hadn't been in the bathroom so where was she?

He switched on all the lights and called her name, quietly because if she were somewhere near he did not wish her to know the panic he was in. It was absurd but he was afraid without knowing what he was afraid of.

'Gina? Gina?'

Silence answered him. He got up and self-consciously looked in the big wardrobe. Yet even as he opened the door, he knew she would not be hiding in there – hiding anywhere, in fact. It was a long time since Gina had played any childish jokes on him.

He ran downstairs wondering if she could have slipped past the sitting-room door into the kitchen without him noticing – but the place was deserted. Really worried now, he went upstairs two at a time to see if it was possible that she had packed a suitcase and left. At the top of the stairs a sixth sense made him aware that the spare room door was ajar. He paused, uneasiness growing and with it a certainty that he would find her in there. Drawing a deep breath, he pushed open the door and switched on the light.

Gina was curled up on the carpet, her head resting on her arms on the nursing chair that stood by the empty cot she had bought for Linda. She was fast asleep.

Relief at seeing her gave way to anger. He stepped forward and shook her by the shoulders. She stirred, opened her eyes, and taking him completely aback, she gave him a warm sensuous smile.

'Hullo, darling!' she said huskily.

She was wearing a matching yellow nylon nightdress and negligee which had been his last Christmas present to her. With her red hair, the colour suited her perfectly and now, in the shaded glow of the nursery lamp, her soft round body showed through the thin material causing Charles to forget his anger in a sudden desperate desire to lift her and carrying her back to their double bed. He bent on one knee beside her but as he did so, the smile began to fade from her eyes and she blinked sleepily.

'What's the matter? What's wrong?'

He realized she was only half awake and his voice now gentle, said:

'You're in the wrong room, Gina. It's half past eleven. Did you fall asleep in here? What happened?'

'I came in to … to…' she broke off, her eyes going from Charles' face around the room and back to Charles. She ended flatly, 'I came in to find something and must have

131

fallen asleep.'

The explanation satisfied him and he put a hand on her soft white arm and tried not to notice that her body pulled away from him.

'Let me carry you back to bed, darling!' he said huskily. 'You'll catch cold here.'

She stood up quickly and shook her head.

'It's all right – I can manage. Sorry to be so silly.'

She walked past him and back into their bedroom.

Charles followed her uncertainly. He was trying to make himself obey the doctor's commands not to force his own desires on his wife. His instinct told him to go after her and *make* her love him as once long ago he had been able to do. But reason accepted the medical opinion he had sought. Better to be patient and wait. Tomorrow, maybe … he must do everything he could to make the day perfect.

'Like a hot drink, darling?' he asked. 'Cocoa – Ovaltine?'

She nodded and he went down to the kitchen to make it. When he went back to their room, she was fast asleep, her face childishly innocent and uncomplicated, utterly unaware of its sensuous appeal to the man she had married and who stood watching her – and wanting desperately what he had put beyond his reach.

9

Gina looked at the Victoria Station clock and noted that it was exactly five past ten. The train was on time and she could follow her usual time-table exactly. She shouldered her way past the crowds jostling around her and went into the cafeteria.

Here, too, there were a great many people. Gina joined the queue at the self-service counter and presently bought herself a cup of coffee. She looked calm, poised and well-dressed – to an onlooker, much like any other housewife come up to London for a day's shopping.

But inside, Gina was trembling with excitement. *It could be today! It could happen today!* The thought beat inside her head like a catchy tune, the phrases repeating themselves over and over again.

She chose a table in the centre of the room from where she could see most of the other occupants, and sat down. Before touching her coffee, she opened her handbag and drew out a left-luggage ticket. She knew the number by heart now, BX 7592. As on every other morning, she wondered whether the clothes lying inside the deposited suitcase were becoming very creased. It was six weeks now since she had handed in the case. She had not imagined then that it would have to stay there so long. Maybe if she wasn't successful today, she should retrieve the case, take it home and iron the clothes. But she had considered this before and on balance, it was not the best solution. Someone at the village hall might see her with the case and somehow have occasion to tell Charles…

Gina stirred some sugar into her coffee and drank it thoughtfully. Whatever happened, she must not let herself feel sorry for Charles. It was his own fault she intended to leave him – he could have kept her if he'd loved her enough…

This reflection made her dive into her handbag once more and look at the letter which was waiting, complete with stamped envelope, to post to Charles. The first one she had written had been pages long but she had cut it down now to a few simple sentences:

I am going away because it is the only thing to do. I know I am making you unhappy and although I have tried very hard to make something of our life together, I don't seem to be able to do so.

Please do not look for me, Charles. I shan't come back so it would be useless to do so. As soon

134

as I have found somewhere to live, I will write to you and then you can begin divorce proceedings which I expect you will want to do.

I hope you will soon find someone else to love you and make you happy and to give you a family of your own.

It was signed simply with her name.

She thought of Charles coming back to the empty cottage, finding her gone and having to spend an evening searching for her. It would not be until the morning post that he would receive the letter. She felt the usual pang of remorse but cast it quickly aside. There was no alternative. To leave the letter at home every morning was to risk discovery of her plans for she never knew which would be The Day. If Charles arrived home early he would see the letter and question her about it and her whole plan would be ruined. There was no alternative but wait before posting the letter until she knew for sure that she wasn't going back.

She put the unsealed envelope back in her handbag and turned to her coffee. Then she stared round the room. People were coming and going – no one stayed very long. It was not the best place to look but then one never knew... Fate had queer ways of working out its plans.

There were two mothers with their children but the youngest was a toddler... Gina knew she was wasting time here.

She stood up quickly and hurried away on the next step of her journey. She looked very purposeful as she walked down the long underground corridor to the tube trains. She caught one fairly soon to Oxford Street and made her way to Selfridges.

Here, as always, there were a number of prams in the entrance hall. Gina stopped still and gazed at the five babies in them. Three were tiny infants, hardly visible beneath bundles of clothing. The other two must have been eight and six months, she estimated. One smiled at her and held out a pudgy, star-fish hand. Gina's face broke into a radiant smile. She moved closer to the pram and touched the outstretched hand. At once, the fingers closed tight round one of hers and the baby cooed.

'Aren't you lovely!' Gina breathed. The child had a crop of fair curls and enormous blue eyes with an unexpected dark fringe of lashes. He was rosy-cheeked and looked extremely well-cared for. The smile left Gina's face and she stood up stiffly, withdrawing her hand from the baby's grasp and avoiding the appeal in the mischievous eyes.

She was familiar now with this battle that went on inside her head.

'Take him – he's beautiful … just what you want, Gina…'

'You know you made yourself a solemn vow –

only an unwanted child...'

'But how do I know he is wanted?'

'Don't be silly. He's beautifully cared for. Obviously his mother loves him.'

'Then why does she risk leaving him alone here. Anyone might come along and steal him. I wouldn't leave my child alone in a shop.'

'You can see he isn't neglected. His mother will be along presently. You promised, Gina, promised, promised...'

She felt with a shock a movement at her side and a voice said:

'Was he crying? I didn't mean to be gone so long but I had to wait at the stocking counter.'

A girl of Gina's age bent over the baby and straightened the pillow, smiling at Gina as she did so.

Gina forced the words past her lips.

'He's a lovely baby. You must be very proud of him.'

'Oh, he's not mine!' her companion said. 'I'm looking after him because his mother is ill. He is lovely, isn't he? And very advanced for his age. His mother dotes on him – I don't know what she'd do if anything happened to him. Do you know, she interviewed sixteen mother's helps before she'd agree to go into hospital. I suppose I should feel very complimented that she felt she could leave her precious baby in my care. Oh, well, I mustn't hang about, I'm late already. Wave bye-bye, Peter…'

'*There!*' said the voice. '*Suppose you'd broken your promise. That's just the perfect example to show you how WRONG it would have been. That mother might have died from shock if you'd taken him away and then how could you have stood your conscience. Wait — the right one will come. The right one WILL come.*'

'*But I've waited so long…*'

'*Perhaps you aren't looking in the right places. Try somewhere else. It's dangerous to hang around the same shops every day. Someone might notice you — get suspicious…*'

Gina stood uncertainly in the hallway. Maybe she *should* try somewhere else…

She wandered out of the shop and along Oxford Street. There were lots of prams and lots of mothers. She looked into each pram which passed but without any real hope.

Suddenly a voice said:

'Why, Gina, what a nice surprise!'

Gina forced herself to concentrate.

'Oh, Mother! Fancy running into you.'

Gina's mother looked at her anxiously.

'Are you well, darling? You look so *thin*. You haven't got 'flu or anything?'

'No, I'm perfectly well.'

'Well, you don't look it. I shall have to speak to Charles. Which reminds me, darling, you haven't been to see Father and me for weeks. To be quite frank, we've been very hurt about it. Surely you can't be all that busy that you can't spare a day for us?'

'Mother, I'm sorry ... I ... I have been busy. You see, Mark and Ilse are getting married and I've promised to find them a flat. It ... it's proving very difficult. I ... I will come and see you both soon.'

Gina's mother stared at her daughter searchingly and then said:

'Yes, Myra told me about the engagement. She told me you don't go to see her much, either. Is it because of Linda?'

Gina's mouth tightened for a moment and then she shrugged.

'I suppose so. I'm sure you can understand that it's really better if I don't see too much of the child. She was ... she was very dependent on me. Since we aren't going to adopt her, it's best she should transfer her affections elsewhere.'

Mrs Oliver relaxed.

'Well, that does seem a logical way to look at it. Are you lunching with anyone, Gina, or could we lunch together? We could have a nice long talk...'

'I'm sorry, but I can't. I ... I have to meet an agent – a house agent, I mean, in half an hour. He's taking me over a flat at Notting Hill Gate. I may be there some time. I'll ring you, Mother, and fix a day to come and see you.'

'Well, make it soon, Gina. Your father was only saying last night that you'd completely deserted us. After all, we are your parents, Gina, and although I know you're a busy housewife these days, it's not as if you're tied to a family like Myra. You could come, if you wanted to.'

Gina made no reply.

After a few more mild reproaches, Mrs Oliver kissed her daughter good-bye and then continued in the opposite direction. Inside Gina's head, the voice spoke again.

'*She believed you about the agent. It was lucky she didn't ask why you weren't carrying any house particulars. Soon you'll really have to spend a day house-hunting.*'

'*No, I won't ... it'll happen soon – today. It has to happen today.*'

'*So you believe in Fate ... then leave it to Fate. Here's an Underground. Take a ticket somewhere – try somewhere new ... anywhere...*'

'Where to, miss?'

She glanced at the man in the ticket office and then up at the directions board and said quickly:

'Swiss Cottage!'

It was the first name to catch her eye. In the train, she felt a mounting excitement following the depression caused by the meeting with her mother. Swiss Cottage. It was quite unfamiliar – she'd only looked in the heart of London so far. Maybe this was Fate at work, guiding her to the one place where...

'Excuse me, miss, is this right for Neasden?'

Gina turned her head and focussed her eyes on the untidy woman who had spoken from behind her.

'I … I'm afraid I don't know.'

'I'm sure it isn't the right train … oh, dear, I'd better ask someone else. Oh, do be quiet, Angela!'

She pulled the little girl's legs so that she collapsed from a kneeling position at the window into a sitting position. On the other side of the child was a boy, maybe a year younger, very grubby and as unkempt as his sister, silently chewing gum. In the woman's arms was a small baby, wrapped in a torn, faintly dirty shawl. She shifted the child on to her other arm and shrugged wearily.

'Kids! Who'd have them! *Will* you sit still, Angela!'

Gina felt her heart jolt.

As casually as she could she leant over and looked at the sleeping baby. Its face was as dirty as the other children's and far from appealing. The voice said:

'Yes, but it … it's so dirty … and not very pretty…'

'You can clean it, and it's very young – it'll be much prettier when it's well fed and fills out a bit…'

'How old is the baby?'

'Nine weeks!' The mother grimaced. 'Been

more trouble than all the others put together. Don't know what's wrong with him – cries all night and sleeps all day. Honestly, I'm at my wit's end to know what to do with him nights.'

'*All* the others? You mean these two?'

'Oh, no, I've two more at home. My neighbour's looking after them. I've five altogether under six. The two between the baby and Arthur here are twins. I've told my husband straight I'm not having no more. Trouble is, you see...' she said, leaning towards Gina in a confidential manner: 'My husband's Irish and an R.C. His religion won't allow family planning. But I've seen my doctor about it and he's going to try to get me fixed up – so I don't have any more.'

She glanced at Gina and saw that her audience was interested. She went on:

'It's all right for some – they know ways to avoid having kids – but me, well, the midwife told me herself that I'm the sort who's only got to have her husband look at her and I'm pregnant. You got any kids?'

Gina shook her head.

'Don't know how lucky you are ... morning, noon and night ... nothing but washing and ironing ... never takes me out dancing...'

The woman's voice droned on and was overshadowed by the voice in Gina's head, saying:

'Hurry, you may not have much time. This is IT – she'll be GLAD to have you take the baby. Of course, it may be a shock at first, but when she gets over it, she'll be so pleased and glad. And you can take such care of him … love him so much…'

She glanced quickly at the map. Where were they? Kilburn – only three more stops to Neasden. She said:

'You did say you were going to Neasden?'

The woman stopped talking and said agitatedly:

'Yes, yes, I did. Oh, I do hope this is the right train. I meant to ask but…'

'It is all right. I must have been dreaming when you asked me earlier. You see, I'm going to Neasden myself.'

Her companion gave a sigh of relief.

'Oh, well, we can relax then.' She paused to yank the small boy back on to the seat and to pull the little girl, Angela, down from the window. Her movements were automatic and irritable. 'Honestly, I feel like giving up sometimes. I've told my husband if I don't get a holiday away from them for a bit, I'll go out of my mind. Do you know…'

'Don't rush things!' said the voice in Gina's head. *'You'll spoil everything if you aren't very, very careful, calm and careful.'*

'You aren't feeding the baby yourself?' she asked, touching the edge of the grubby shawl and looking into the baby's sleeping face.

'Lord, no! He's on National Dried. That's what all mine were reared on and I haven't never had a moment's trouble with any of them until this one. Proper nuisance, he is...'

Gina wasn't listening. She was too relieved to know that the baby was bottle-fed. If his mother had been feeding him, then all her hopes would have been dashed.

'Neasden! Neasden!'

Gina jumped up and held out her arms.

'Let me carry him for you,' she said.

'Ta, thanks!' The woman handed over the baby, a little surprised but grateful. She lifted her shopping bag and grabbed the younger boy by the hand and followed Gina on to the platform, Angela clinging to her coat.

'That's the way out!' Gina said. 'I'll lead the way, shall I?'

She began to stride ahead, mingling with the people who were also getting off at the Neasden stop and those who were hurrying to catch the train before its doors closed.

She did not turn her head to see if the woman was following. She knew that she must be gaining distance – the little boy could certainly not keep up at the pace she was going.

She turned suddenly into a side tunnel saying UP TRAINS. Her breath was coming quickly now and she paused for an instant, daring herself to glance over her shoulder. No one was following her. She hurried forward and found herself on the opposite platform. Almost at once a train drew in.

'Baker Street train!' shouted the coloured porter.

A smile of relief crossed Gina's face as she hurried in through the open doors. Fate was handing her all the cards. It had happened at last – it was Her Day, the Moment she had waited for so impatiently for the last two months…

In the train, she pulled back the shawl from the baby's face and stared down at it. It was still sleeping. She longed to wash the tiny face and put on new clothes – well, it wouldn't be so long now. She had a complete set of baby clothes in the suitcase – they would be a little large for this baby – but she could buy others tomorrow. These she would burn leaving no trace of his past.

Her weeks of planning were paying dividends now. At Baker Street she changed trains for Victoria and there she collected her suitcase and posted the letter to Charles.

It was now lunch-time. The baby was awake and becoming restless. Gina went into the ladies' room and opened her suitcase and got out a bottle and teat. She found the attendant and asked her to hold the child while she went into the chemist next door to buy some milk. When the bottle was made up, she went back to the ladies' room and tipped the attendant before settling down to feed the child.

He was hungry and took the bottle, despite the new teat, without any difficulty. Gina relaxed. She had, she realized, been living on the edge of her nerves for the last two hours. Now there was only one last worry – digs...

She took a taxi to the end of the road in Bloomsbury where the residential hotel she had already visited twice, was situated. She walked the last twenty yards, her arms aching with the weight of the child on one arm and the suitcase on the other.

She rang the bell, her heart beating with nervous tension. A grey-haired woman with spectacles and a tired, lined face, opened the door to her.

'Oh, it's you, Miss Wood. You'd better come in.'

'Is the job still going? I'm sorry I couldn't come last week.'

The landlady sighed.

'The job's going all right. There aren't that many these days want domestic work – only foreign girls and I don't think much to them, I can tell you.'

Gina followed her into her private office.

'Your room's clean but the bed's not made up. Pity you couldn't let me know before!' The woman gave Gina a sharp glance. She

146

was still a little suspicious. Girls with Gina's background didn't usually go in for menial domestic work – not unless they'd been in trouble. Still, at least this girl had been frank about it – run away from home, had an illegitimate baby and now had to support it. Part of her respectable upbringing condemned Gina but the other more womanly half approved of the girl's willingness to keep her child and make some sort of life for it.

'The work's hard, I don't pretend it isn't. You're sure you want the job?'

'Yes, yes, I'm quite sure!'

'Very well then. Five pounds a week and two half days, Wednesday and Sunday.'

The woman looked at the bundle in Gina's arms. The baby was now in clean clothes, had been washed and was obviously well-cared for. She softened.

'You never said if it was a boy or girl.'

'Boy! His name is Michael.'

'There, the little pet. He's quite well now?'

'Oh, yes, he's fine. It's wonderful having him back – I hated leaving him at the hospital but I suppose it was for the best. He's quite well now – it was the not knowing when I could have him back that made it awkward. I didn't know until this morning they were going to discharge him.'

'Well, let's hope he keeps fit now. I'll show you up to your room and then you can settle in. I shan't need you before supper – you'll have to lay the tables then and help serve. Supper is at seven and unless any of them are late, you should be washed up and breakfast laid by eight-thirty. Then your time's your own.'

She looked at Gina's thin pale face with some misgivings.

'I hope you're stronger than you look,' she said anxiously. 'It's a job as will keep you on your feet. Up at six-thirty, early morning teas and calls, then breakfast and after that the rooms to do out. You'll have a half-hour mid-morning break and then lunch to lay and serve and help wash up. You think you can manage – with him, I mean?'

She nodded at the baby.

'Oh, yes, I'm sure. He's a very good baby, sleeps all day. I'm sure I'll manage. Thank you very much, Mrs Wheatly, for giving me the chance.'

'Well, that's all right – glad to have your help. And you'd best call me Ma'am, otherwise Cook will be giving in her notice. You'll have to go careful with her – a bit temperamental – Irish. But you strike me as the quiet sort – she prefers your kind. Well, we'll go up, then.'

Gina tried not to notice the shabby, dingy atmosphere of the hotel, as Mrs Wheatly called it. Really, it was more like a boarding house. The air smelt stale and it was dark, chilly and depressing. But on the top floor, though her room was small, it was filled with afternoon sunshine and Gina's heart lifted.

As soon as her employer had gone, she sat down on the narrow unmade bed and leant on her elbows, staring down at the baby, still sleeping in the folds of the soft creamy shawl. He looked very different now from the grubby little bundle on the train to Neasden – almost unrecognizable. Soon it would be possible to forget that he had ever belonged to such a mother.

'Michael? Michael?' she whispered.

The baby stirred, lifted a small clenched fist against his tiny rosebud mouth, and gave a hiccough, then settled back to sleep. Gina's heart melted in tenderness. Her baby – at last, she had her very own baby. She'd work so hard for him – love him so much. Maybe five pounds a week was not a fortune but with everything 'found', as Mrs Wheatly had put it, it would be enough to buy all Michael's needs. This afternoon she would buy a pram. Two days ago she'd seen the very thing she needed – a karri-cot which fitted inside a pram frame, so doing double duty. It was in excellent condition, although second-hand and she had enough money in her handbag to pay for it.

She opened her bag and carefully counted the notes inside. Twenty-three pounds.

There were also five half-crowns. She'd saved so carefully from the housekeeping money Charles had allowed her…

Charles! She glanced at her watch and saw that it was only four o'clock. In two hours' time Charles would arrive home – find her gone. Poor Charles!

Maybe he would phone her parents. Mother would say she'd seen Gina in Oxford Street – well, that wouldn't be much help to him. He would never, never find her here.

Gina smiled faintly and began to make up her bed. The baby slept on. The night was still to come. But she wasn't in the least worried. Everything that had happened today only proved to her that at long last Fate was working for her, guiding her footsteps to the Neasden train, engineering the meeting with the baby's mother, even down to the last important detail of ensuring the job and a home was still open to her.

'We're lucky, Michael, my precious baby!' she said and stopped to hug the child tightly in her starved arms.

To Michael's mother, she never gave another thought.

10

Charles was furious. He'd been late home after a long, tiring day and yet again, Gina was not there to welcome him. There was no dinner cooking in the oven, nothing ready for him. It was really too bad. What was more, it was the last time it would happen. He'd put a stop to this house-hunting game of Gina's, once and for all.

He poured himself a sherry and mooched round the cottage trying to find something to occupy him until Gina's return. It was nearly seven o'clock – the latest she had been so far. His irritation mounted.

At seven-thirty, he began to worry. Could anything have happened to her? She was so vague and dreamy these days. Suppose she'd got on a wrong train – gone to Eastbourne or somewhere equally improbable. He never doubted that she had been in London all day.

He thought angrily about Gina's behaviour yesterday. He'd driven her down to the coast, happy and grateful because it was a gloriously sunny day – just right for the picnic he'd planned on the South Downs. He'd chatted happily to her until he realized

she was making no effort to talk back to him
– that her replies were mere monosyllables.
It was the same during lunch – the same
after lunch when they had gone into
Brighton and on the pier. She'd never once
smiled, never opened a conversation, never
showed any sign of enjoying herself the way
he'd hoped she would. His own good spirits
had become slowly dampened until they
petered out into a morose silence. It was like
taking out a damp squib, he'd told himself.
Gina was not only no fun but a dead loss.

As he drove her home he'd tried to recap-
ture the gay mood of anticipation with which
he had begun the day. She looked pale and
tired but infinitely desirable sitting beside
him, her delicate profile clearly visible in the
moonlight. He'd pressed her hand in his and
said urgently:

'You have enjoyed yourself a little, haven't
you, darling?'

'Oh, yes, thank you!'

His hopes rose.

'You're so quiet, Gina. Talk to me.'

'I … I don't know what to talk about.'

She did not withdraw her hand from his
and he took this as a sign of encouragement.

'We'll be home soon – unless you'd like to
stop on Devil's Dyke and look at the moon?'

She nodded her head – neither an assent
nor a dissent.

Charles had decided to drive straight

home. At least if Gina wasn't in a negative mood, there was a chance that...

'I'll make a hot drink for you, darling, while you're getting ready for bed – provided, of course, that you won't fall asleep before I come up with it like last night.'

'Did I? I'm sorry!'

He dropped a kiss on her head and watched her walk slowly up the stairs. Part of his mind was still worried about her – the change in her was so marked – but the more immediate thought was of his ever-increasing desire for her. If they could only make love, he was sure whatever invisible barrier lay between them, would be vanquished once and for all.

She was not asleep when he carried up the cup of Ovaltine.

He undressed quickly while she was sipping it, and then took the empty cup from her and sat down on the edge of the bed.

'Gina,' he said softly. 'Won't you tell me what's wrong?'

Her eyes, which had been staring into his, dropped swiftly. She said vaguely:

'It must be getting late, Charles. I'm tired.'

'Gina, I want an answer. Are you angry with me about anything? If so, for goodness' sake say so and I'll apologize. I hate this feeling I have of being shut away from you. What *is* wrong, darling?'

She did not answer and Charles' voice

became less gentle and persuasive and more irritable.

'If you won't tell me, how in hell can I do anything about it? Damn it all, I do try to please you. I wanted today to be fun for both of us but judging by your behaviour, I think it was a complete waste of time. You're sulking about something – about Linda, I suppose. Well, I've just about had it, Gina. It's months since we agreed to let the child go and live with Myra. It's a bit late now to start blaming me for not wanting her here.'

'I – I don't mind about Linda – not now!'

He had been startled into momentary silence. Then he said:

'Then if it's not Linda, *what is it?*'

But she would not answer and her silence drove him back to an angry hurt attack.

'I've had enough of it. It's just not fair to me. You seem to forget I'm your husband. What do you suppose it's like, coming home every night to sullen stares and incomprehensible silences? No joke, I can tell you. It's not even as if you'll let me make love to you any more.'

Again she surprised him.

'I haven't refused!'

He caught his breath and replied sharply:

'All right, but you can't say you've been very encouraging either, let alone eager.'

'We'll do it now if you want…'

He nearly struck her.

154

'You talk as if you were willing to do me a favour.' He mimicked her voice. 'We'll do it now if you want! Can't you understand, Gina? I don't want to make love to you if you don't want me to. You don't, do you?'

'You can if you want.'

Too angry to reply, he stood up and stared down at her, hating her in this moment of frustration because she looked so soft and feminine and appealing and yet was none of these things deep inside.

'You're out of your mind if you think I'd touch you now,' he said bitterly. 'I'm not an animal – I don't just want a woman– I wanted you … you the way you used to be. Oh, go to sleep. I just don't care any more.'

But he had cared. He'd been deeply hurt because she had made no attempt to call him back into their bedroom. Hurt and humiliated because Gina had let him know her physical desire for him was dead. He no longer believed it was just a matter of health – he felt instinctively the change in her mental attitude to him and knew that she didn't love him any more than she wanted him.

When he finally went back to their room, Gina was asleep. He had lain awake a further hour, puzzled, uneasy, frustrated, until at last sheer exhaustion overcame him and he, too, fell asleep.

Remembering last night, Charles felt all

his anger renewing itself. This time, Gina had really gone too far. If it was her way of hurting him, then it was a damned selfish way and he wasn't going to stand for it.

But as the clock hands moved slowly round to eight, the anger became concern for Gina's safety. He phoned the station to enquire if there had been any delays in trains from London. There had been none. He swallowed his pride and telephoned Myra, asking if perhaps Gina were with her.

'No, she hasn't been here for a week or more. What's happened, Charles? Have you two had a row?'

'Not exactly, though you couldn't very well say we've been on good terms lately. Frankly, I'm worried, Myra. Have you any idea at all where she could be?'

'Maybe she found a flat at last and has stayed up in Town to show Mark. Shall I give Mark's digs a ring? Maybe he'll know where she is.'

'Okay, Myra, thanks. Ring me back at once, won't you?'

Ten minutes later Myra telephoned back to say that she had spoken to Mark who hadn't heard from Gina or seen her since two weekends ago at Myra's house.

'I phoned Mother and Father – just in case. But Gina isn't there, either. Mother says she saw her in Oxford Street and wanted to lunch with her, but Gina was dashing off to meet a house agent and seemed busy so they only talked for a few minutes. I'm sure she must be on her way back by now. Ring me at once if she comes in, Charles.'

Charles poured himself a stiff whiskey and sat down to wait. But the silence and inactivity got on his nerves. On a sudden impulse, he phoned the Home where Gina had worked. Matron answered him and, surprised by his question, told him she hadn't seen Gina in months. Charles thanked her quickly and rang off before she began asking him awkward questions. It was bad enough that Myra and Gina's parents should know Gina was playing him up – he was damned if he would let himself be humiliated into asking anyone else.

He had another whiskey and then phoned Myra again.

'She's still not back. Something *must* have happened to her. Do you think I should ring the police?'

There was a pause before Myra said:

'I'll ask Malcolm what he thinks.'

Charles' hand clenched round the receiver. For the first time in his life he was up against something he could not deal with. Most problems had a simple solution but now he was way out of his depth. He was not sure whether anger or concern were uppermost.

Myra's voice spoke into his ear.

'Malcolm says he thinks you could wait a

little while – if there'd been an accident, you would have been notified. Gina must have had some kind of identification in her handbag. Perhaps she's just gone to a late film, Charles. Give her a little while longer.'

Charles rang off. His instinct was for action rather than inaction. He had another whiskey and began to feel less worried and more angry. If Gina had been to a cinema, he'd really lam into her when she got home. This wasn't just a question of being vague and forgetful – it was deliberately designed to hurt him...

But, argued a voice inside him, Gina had never yet allowed her feelings to take a positive form. That was the root of the trouble between them. If she'd complained – told him in words what she had against him – why she'd stopped loving him, he could have dealt with the situation. But there had been no rows, no angry words, far less any kind of provocative action from Gina that would let him get to grips with the problem.

For the first time, Charles began to wonder if Gina had walked out on him. Maybe she'd had enough of their marriage and just packed up and gone. Maybe there was a letter for him on the dressing table – the mantelpiece, which he'd overlooked...

He raced upstairs and searched their bedroom. No letter. He flung open the wardrobe and stared at her clothes. As far as he could see, everything was there. On the chair by the bed was a pair of nylon stockings, her dressing-gown behind the bathroom door, her nightdress neatly folded beneath the pillow. There was not one sign of a hasty departure, of things sorted or packed in a hurry.

He felt a little calmer as he went back downstairs. Gina hadn't left him – that much he was fairly certain about. She'd be back soon. She'd have to be back soon – the last train got in at 10.45.

He sat down to wait the last half-hour. Myra phoned and he spoke to her more calmly, assuring her that he now felt certain Gina would be on the last train.

'But I don't understand, Charles. *Why* do this without warning you? What's the point?'

'To show me how independent she is!'

There was a pause and then Myra said:

'But why?'

Charles hunched his shoulders. Psychology was not one of his strong points.

'How should I know? Personally, I think she's never really forgiven me about Linda. I know she agreed at the time that it was best for Linda to come to you, but I think she's been secretly nursing a grudge against me. We were perfectly happy until she got this obsession about Linda.'

Myra said:

'It doesn't sound like Gina – to go around

159

nursing a secret grudge. She's always been an extrovert, Charles – even as a little girl she'd pour out her troubles, lose her temper, burst into tears. We all knew just what was wrong with Gina.'

'Well, I wish you knew what was wrong with her now,' Charles said moodily. 'I can't deal with her. I've tried to be patient but this is about the last straw. I'm beginning to think I don't care whether she comes back or not!'

He didn't really believe what he was saying but it was some comfort to hear Myra's shocked voice begging him to remember that Gina hadn't been well, that maybe she needed medical treatment– Charles mustn't on any account stop loving her – he was all Gina had.

'Well, it doesn't seem as if she appreciates me much!' Charles said childishly, but mollified all the same. 'We'll see when she gets back.'

But Gina did not come back and after eleven o'clock and another telephone conversation with Myra and Malcolm, Charles telephoned the police.

The police were sympathetic but not apparently very worried. Obviously they looked upon Gina's disappearance as a typical marital tiff. She'd turn up next day. Meanwhile, they'd had no report from the hospitals so she couldn't have had an accident.

'But suppose she has lost her memory? She hasn't been at all well lately – very vague and almost as if she were half asleep.'

'Even if she can't identify herself, there'll be something on her – in her handbag, for instance. You say she went up to London, didn't you, sir? No doubt, she bought a return ticket – so for a start, they'll know she comes from this village. Aren't any other young ladies answering her description reported missing so stands to reason we'll know it's her when they make enquiries. If you could nip down in your car, sir, and give us a description and a photo if you have one?'

It was midnight when Charles got home. He was tired, cold and hungry. His head ached from too many whiskeys on an empty stomach. He cut himself a large cheese sandwich but couldn't eat it. The sensible thing now was to go to bed but he knew he wouldn't sleep. He sat down in his armchair and tried not to notice how silent the room was, how empty the house without Gina. He stared into the unlit fire and wondered how he would get through the seven or eight hours till morning when he might reasonably expect word from the police. As he sat there wondering, he was suddenly overcome by nervous exhaustion combined with alcohol and it was not until the milkman banged on the door at seven o'clock that he woke up.

He was cold, stiff and his head ached furiously. He was appalled that he could have slept with so much on his mind. Then the phone rang and he raced to it, believing the police had traced her. But it was Myra saying she was on her way round. She couldn't stand the lack of news any longer.

Charles was glad to see his sister-in-law. He was glad to be told by someone what to do. Myra made him bath and shave and while he was dressing, cooked him a hot breakfast. He was eating it when the second knock on the front door heralded the postman. Myra gathered up the letters and gave them to Charles – two bills and a letter.

'Gina's handwriting!' Charles exclaimed. Suddenly his hands were trembling and he looked at Myra unbelievingly. 'I … I don't want to open it,' he said.

'Come on, Charles, we have to know where she is – what she's doing. Open it.'

He did so, reading the words without really comprehending them. He looked at the postmark on the envelope and handed it together with the letter to Myra.

'I think she's left me – for good!' he said.

Myra read the letter twice and sat down suddenly.

'I just don't understand. Why didn't she tell me if this was the way she felt? Why didn't she tell you? And where has she gone?

She must have been planning this for ages. What *has* gone wrong?'

Charles pushed away his half empty plate and put his head in his hands.

'I've failed to make her happy, I suppose,' he said bitterly. 'God knows, I tried, Myra. We were happy – at first. I'll swear it has something to do with Linda – she never forgave me because I didn't want to adopt the child. But how could I when I didn't feel anything towards the child except pity?'

Myra looked at him sympathetically.

'I tried to explain your point of view to her – and I think she understood. Are you sure it's Linda? Maybe it has something to do with Mark and Ilse...'

Charles looked up quickly and Myra wished the words unsaid.

'You mean she was in love with Mark? Maybe she still is in love with him?'

'No, I didn't mean that. But that day Mark and Ilse got engaged – do you remember? Gina made one very poignant remark – she told Ilse Mark was a wonderful person and that *he'd make a wonderful father.*'

Charles' face was even more bitter.

'And so might I have made a good father. It wasn't *my* fault we couldn't have children. As a matter of fact, I was pretty disappointed when she told me we couldn't. But damn it all, Myra, children aren't the reason we got married. We were in love – we wanted to share our lives, be together. Doesn't that count for anything with Gina? I tried to make her see children didn't matter all that much to me – not so long as I had her. Wasn't that the right thing to do?'

'Yes, I'm sure it was!' Myra agreed. 'But maybe in the end it just wasn't enough for Gina. Maybe if you could have agreed to adopt a baby...'

Charles was silent. He *had* been definite enough about not wanting to adopt a child – but then it would have been wrong to pretend a feeling he didn't have. He'd always been convinced he'd never care for someone else's unwanted child and Linda had proved his point. All the same, Gina had begged him to try – she'd said something about a period of trial lasting three, or was it six months? He hadn't really listened. Maybe he should have agreed at least to try so that she could see for herself that it wasn't going to work.

'Dash it all, Myra, I wasn't being selfish about it. I wasn't against Gina having a baby – of our own. It was just the idea of adoption...'

'Well, it doesn't seem to matter now,' Myra said sadly. 'Gina's gone. I wish she'd let me know – she must be so unhappy, so alone.'

Charles stood up, his face determined.

'You don't think I'm going to let her go

just like that! She's got to be found, Myra, and then we'll get this all sorted out. The police said last night she shouldn't be hard to trace. Wherever she's gone, she can be found. If necessary, I'll employ a private detective. People can't just vanish into thin air...'

He snatched the letter back from Myra and read it again. He covered the deep hurt with anger.

'She can't do this to me!' he said dramatically. 'She's my wife and I say she's to come home, I'm going down to the police station. She just can't do this to me...'

A moment later Myra heard his car start up and she sighed and went into the sitting room to phone Malcolm.

11

She was too busy trying to cope with her new job and the baby to read the papers. Three dailies carried the same comparatively small item of news:

'Baby kidnapped at Neasden Underground– At three-fifteen yesterday afternoon, a young attractive woman in her twenties, walked off with the seven-week-old baby of Mr and Mrs Patrick O'Hallihan, of 3 Pirbright Terrace, Neasden. Mrs O'Hallihan told police that the young woman had offered to carry the baby as they left the train and had then disappeared into the crowds on the platform. The police have asked the press to help trace the woman who was dressed in a smart green tweed costume, a white polo-necked jersey. The woman, thought to be about twenty-five years old, had red hair, grey eyes and was well spoken. The baby had on a white dress, yellow cardigan and was wrapped in a cream wool and nylon shawl. Anyone who has seen this woman is asked to get in touch with the nearest police station.'

Gina's landlady was puzzled. The description of the woman fitted Gina perfectly but the baby Gina had brought with her was dressed all in blue. She thought of going up to the girl's room to question her more closely but decided against it. If Gina *was* the wanted woman the police were after, she might do a bolt. And the fact was, she needed the girl badly. Domestic help was hard enough to get and the place was far too big for her to manage on her own. She'd felt she'd done very well to get a girl as decent as Gina wanting such a job but then, as she told her neighbour later in the day over a cup of tea, 'those as had done wrong weren't in a position to pick and choose their jobs'. Gina had confessed the baby was illegitimate which explained why she was willing to take on such menial tasks.

'*If* it is illegitimate!' said the landlady darkly, 'Or maybe kidnapped!'

She decided to do nothing for a day or two. Despite her secret convictions, she told herself that maybe it was some other woman like Gina, who had taken the baby. She bought an evening paper and read it carefully to see if the baby had been found. She scanned the following morning paper but there was only another plea to the public to come forward if they had seen the wanted woman and a tear-jerking appeal from its real mother to '*send my baby back*'. The landlady sniffed at the picture of the untidy mother outside her terraced home with her other children gathered round her.

'With that lot to look after, shouldn't think she'd miss one!' she told her neighbour over elevenses. But the friend was more sentimental.

'Think what that poor woman must feel, not knowing if her baby is alive or dead. After all, it's her own flesh and blood – and only seven weeks old. Have you said anything to the girl yet?'

The landlady shook her head.

'Not about this!' she flicked the paper with her hand. 'She's a good worker – I wouldn't want to lose her. All the same, I suppose it's my duty. Yet somehow, I can't associate her with a crime like kidnapping – she's so quiet and respectable. I mean, why should she do a thing like that? It doesn't make sense.'

'Maybe she lost her own baby – women do go funny sometimes after they've lost a child. There was a film on telly not so long ago about a woman like that who refused to believe her own baby had died and she took this other woman's. Mad, she was!'

'Well, my girl certainly isn't mad. She's picked up the job very quickly and the guests like her; she's polite and helpful. I don't want to lose her.'

In the end, the two women decided to say nothing to Gina but to voice their suspicions . to the police. They hoped to make the enquiries discreetly. Then, if it was all a mistake and Gina not involved, she'd be able to stay on without any ill feeling towards her employer.

The police sergeant was interested and phoned his superior for instructions. They sent the landlady and her neighbour home and began their enquiries.

Gina was putting Michael to bed when the policewoman called. She was feeling so physically exhausted that it was a full minute before she realized the implications of having a policewoman in the room.

The baby had kept her awake most of the last two nights. The fact that he slept through the day had not helped since she had been so busy with her domestic work that there had been no chance to catch up on lost sleep. There were nappies to wash, feeds to make up and behind everything, a constant nagging worry that the child wasn't well. He was frequently sick and her instinct rather than experience gained at the Home, told her his food was not suiting him and that she ought to get medical advice. But to do so was to risk someone finding out the baby was not hers.

'I have some questions I would like to ask you Miss Wood. May I come in?'

Gina nodded. She must try to pull herself together, to think quickly, give the right answers.

'This is your baby?' The policewoman

walked to Michael's cot and looked in. Gina nodded.

'Perhaps you would like to tell me when and where he was born? You see, Miss Wood, we have no child registered in that name in the last seven weeks. It is, of course, legally necessary to register a child within a few weeks of its birth.'

Gina had not expected this question; had no answer to it. She looked from Michael to the policewoman and then, despairingly, down at her hands.

'Perhaps you would prefer not to answer any more questions until you have your solicitor present?'

'Are you arresting me?' Gina asked desperately.

'No! I am simply making enquiries. But I do have to ask you to come down to the police station with me. There is a car and driver outside. I think you had better bring the baby with you. We can straighten everything out at the station.'

'Are you going to take Michael away from me?'

The policewoman saw the agony in Gina's eyes and her official manner gave way to a gentle, womanly concern.

'Try not to worry about that now. Get your coat and hat and I'll help you with the karri-cot.'

Gina sat dry-eyed on the short trip to the

police station. Despite the gentle voice and kindly manner of her companion, she knew that she was going to lose Michael – that he would be given back to that woman in the train. Beyond this fact, her mind refused to function. She was not afraid of what would happen to her – the thought simply did not occur to her that she was now in serious trouble. Nothing mattered except that they would be taking Michael away and that there was nothing she could do to stop them.

At the police station she was given a cup of tea. The policewoman took Michael into another room. When she came back a few minutes later, the baby was not with her. She put an arm round Gina's shoulders and told her to drink her tea – it was getting cold. Then a police officer came up and said:

'We have reason to believe that the child in your possession is Patrick Gary O'Hallihan, and that you took this child from his mother at approximately three-fifteen on Tuesday, 18th of September, 1963, at Neasden Underground Station. Do you deny this charge? You are not obliged to answer but I must warn you that I have the child's mother in the next room and she has identified the baby as her own.'

'Yes, I took him!' Gina whispered. 'She didn't really want him – she said she had enough children already – and I wanted him so much. I – I called him Michael.'

But the policeman had disappeared and the policewoman beside her said gently:

'Would you like to phone for your solicitor? I'm afraid you will be arrested formally now that you have admitted taking the baby. You do have a solicitor?'

Gina shook her head. The only solicitor she knew of was the man Charles had engaged when they were buying the cottage – and she couldn't contact him without Charles knowing what she had done. She didn't want Charles to know – he wouldn't understand. He'd be so angry and she couldn't stand that.

The policeman was back, his voice interrupting her thoughts... '...*not bound to say anything ... anything you do say will be used in evidence...*'

Then the policewoman was taking her to a cell.

It was quite clean and not uncomfortable. Gina lay down on the bed and asked:

'Has he gone? Michael? Has she taken him away?'

'Yes, his mother has taken him home.'

'What will happen now?' Gina's voice was leaden, not really interested in the future. Nothing mattered any more. Nothing.

'You'll be brought up before the Magistrate tomorrow morning at the Magistrates' Court and he will decide what is to be done.

Have you any relatives or friends with whom you would like to get in touch? Angela Wood is not your real name, is it?'

Gina shook her head.

'Then you will have to give your real name.'

Again Gina shook her head.

'I can't!' she whispered. 'I don't want my husband – my family to know.'

The policewoman looked at her anxiously. There had been nothing in Gina's handbag or possessions she carried to identify her.

They would, of course, search her room at the hotel. She was surprised to hear Gina was married. The girl was a bit of a mystery – obviously not the criminal type. She seemed to be in a state of shock – or exhaustion. She tried again to explain to Gina that she was in serious trouble and needed a friend – her husband.

But Gina, realizing at last the possible legal consequences of her actions, refused to say any more. She was given some supper and her night things were brought to her. Then she lay down again on the bed and for the first time in two days, she slept an unbroken sleep.

The policewoman who accompanied Gina to court next morning was surprised at her apparent calm. Gina appeared to be completely disinterested in what was going to happen to her. Her manner was quite composed. She had not wept when the baby was taken from her, nor since. She seemed not to feel anything at all.

'Silence!' called out a policeman at the back of the court.

A door opened at one end of the room and four Justices came in and sat down at a table. The Clerk of the Court answered the Magistrate's request for the first case. He called out Gina's fictitious name and it was a moment or two before she realized they were calling for her. Then the policewoman at her side gave her a push and she went forward to sit down in the chair opposite the Magistrate.

'Angela Wood, you are charged that on September the 18th of this year at Neasden Underground Station you did take an infant, Patrick Gary O'Hallihan from his mother. Do you plead guilty or not guilty?'

Gina looked from the Clerk to the Magistrate and back to the Clerk.

'Guilty!' she said quietly.

'Is she legally represented?' the Magistrate asked after a long look at Gina.

'No, your Worship!' It was the police officer from the station who had formally arrested her the previous evening. 'The accused gave a false name, refused to give her real name or to call a solicitor.'

'Very well. You may give your evidence!'

Gina heard the man take the oath and then

174

give an account of what had transpired the previous evening. She stopped listening, not wanting to hear about Michael's mother being called to identify her child. The policeman called him Patrick but Gina thought of him still as Michael. She tried *not* to think of him. She tried to make her mind a blank until the policeman's last words caught her attention.

'Her husband is here to speak for her.'

Charles – Charles here? She looked quickly round the room, seeing the reporters for the first time; then Charles as he strode purposefully from the back of the room towards the witness box.

But Charles was only allowed to give her real name. Then the Magistrate turned to Gina and said gently:

'Mrs Martin? Will you tell me why you took the child? I understand from the evidence we have just heard that the mother was a stranger to you? What made you take her baby from her?'

Gina frowned and wondered how it was possible to explain.

'Well?'

'I … I wanted him!'

'You have no children of your own?'

'No!' Her voice was barely audible.

'Surely you realized you would be doing a very wrong – indeed a criminal thing taking this child away from its mother and trying to pass it off as your own?'

'She already had four children and she hadn't wanted him. I wouldn't have taken Michael from her if she'd wanted him. And you see, I'd been looking for a baby for so long.'

The Magistrate turned to confer with the other Justices in a whisper. Then he looked at Charles and told him to step forward.

'You were not aware of what your wife was doing?'

'No, your Worship. She left home suddenly three days ago. I've been nearly out of my mind with worry. I reported her missing the night of the 18th when she didn't come home. It was only this morning the police told me Gina – my wife, was in prison. I telephoned at once but there wasn't time to see her before she was due in court here. So I came straight here. Your Worship, I would like very much to talk to her – she's not well. I'm sure she didn't know what she was doing. I ... I'd like to engage a solicitor for her.'

'Very well. I'll remand the case until after lunch. In the meanwhile, I suggest you and your wife see the Probation Officer. I'll continue with this case at 2.15.'

Suddenly they were alone together in the Probation Officer's room. The officer had not yet come in but there was a policeman sitting outside the door – a fact which served to remind Charles that his wife was still a prisoner.

He took a step towards her and said violently:

'My God, Gina, what came over you?'

He tried to put a protective arm round her shoulder but she stepped back from him.

'I don't want to talk about it!' she said, her voice toneless, frightening him. 'I didn't want you to come here – I gave another name but they found out anyway...'

'Gina, I've already telephoned Mr Pilford, that solicitor who did the house searches and so on when we bought the cottage. Will you talk to *him?* He said he'd be here as soon as he could.'

'I don't want to talk to anyone. I haven't any excuse. I – I don't mind going to prison. I'll have to go, won't I?' The thought had only just occurred to her.

Charles was saved a reply by the entrance of the Probation Officer, a kindly, grey-haired woman who smiled at Gina, patted her arm and said briskly:

'Well, now, have you got this unfortunate business straightened out?'

Charles looked at her desperately.

'My wife won't tell me anything. I don't know what to do. I just don't understand it...'

The woman looked at Gina's tense white face and suggested politely but firmly, that

Charles wait outside for a few moments. She would talk to Gina alone.

When Charles had left the room, the Officer introduced herself.

'My name is Whitby, Mrs Whitby. You're Gina Martin, aren't you, and the angry young man who left us is your husband?'

Gina nodded.

Mrs Whitby sat down behind her desk and motioned Gina into the chair opposite her.

'He is young, you know, and a man. Those are probably the two main reasons why he doesn't understand. Why not tell me? I was listening to you in court, you know, and I heard your reason for taking that baby – you wanted him. Have you been wanting a child for a very long time, Gina?'

And suddenly Gina was able to talk. Here, at last, was someone to understand – someone who realized that she had just *had* to take Michael.

'I was going to take care of him – much better than his own mother could. She didn't want him...' The words poured out.

When the story – the whole story of her barrenness and Linda and her illness was told, Gina was crying – not noisily or from self-pity but from relief. So much of her longing had had to be hidden for so long from Charles; hidden deep down inside her being. Now, for the first time, she could speak her thoughts aloud.

'You know, you should have told all this to that young husband of yours – it should never have been bottled up. He would have understood eventually. You just didn't give him time.'

'He had time – all the time Linda was with us; all the time since…'

'No, after Linda went to your sister's, you began to hide your feelings from him because you were afraid of his disapproval. You knew what you were planning was wrong – deep down inside you knew, Gina, but you wouldn't let that part of your mind accept the truth. You schemed and planned and quietened your conscience by telling yourself you would only take an *unwanted* child. You quietened that same voice when it spoke to you of the wrong you would be doing your husband running away from him. You told yourself *he* wouldn't mind because he didn't love you. But that wasn't true, was it? You meant that he didn't love you in your way – giving in to your needs regardless of his own. You have been as selfish as he has been, my dear. But that is not the point at the moment. The question now is how to get you out of the trouble you're in. You do realize, don't you, that it was very, very wrong to take that baby?'

'I … I know it's legally wrong, but he was dirty and uncared for and the mother said she hadn't wanted him…'

'Gina, you must be truthful with *yourself*, even if not with those around you. What the mother may have said is not proof that she failed to love her child. Mothers often say their kids are nothing but a nuisance but they are words, Gina, not feelings. That woman must have suffered untold mental agony wondering what you had done with her baby – if you were caring for him or had murdered him; if she would ever see him again.'

Gina covered her face with her hands. She had been so careful *not* to think about the mother. Mrs Whitby was right – deep down she had been afraid of thinking what that woman might be suffering.

'There are legal ways of obtaining a child – ways such as adoption and fostering that have been carefully thought out so that no one is hurt in the process of handing an unwanted child to a childless woman. You can't circumvent them, Gina, without breaking the law and perhaps breaking a good many hearts as well.'

'But Charles wouldn't…'

'I know. I'm going to speak to him, Gina – try to make him see how essential children are to a happy marriage.'

'Then you do understand?'

'Indeed yes, though I can't approve in any way of what you have done. I had a child once – a little girl of four. Her father was killed in the war and she was all I had. Then she, too, died and I had nothing – no husband to give me more children, no daughter either. At first I thought life wasn't worth living. Then I tried to adopt a child – just as you did, but I learned that women without husbands weren't considered suitable. I was desperate but I couldn't have taken a child as you did, Gina. You see, I had been a mother and I knew all too well what a mother goes through when her child is suddenly taken from her.'

'How awful for you!' Gina said, her own unhappiness momentarily forgotten. To have a husband and child and lose them both…

'It wasn't so awful. I decided to take up probation work. Now I have an unlimited channel of outlet for my maternal feelings. I spend my life mothering people like you. My daughter would have been the same age as you – had she lived.'

Mrs Whitby's conversation with Charles was by no means as difficult as she had feared. Charles was desperate with concern.

'I just never realized how much it all meant to her… I thought she'd get over it. We were so happy together at first – so much in love. I thought it would be enough for her – it was for me. I haven't had a chance to tell her but if she'll come back home, I'll let her have as many children as

181

she wants – adoption or fostering or anything else. We'll try to get Linda back from my sister-in-law if that's the way it has to be. I'll do anything, Mrs Whitby – anything to make her happy.'

'Unfortunately,' said the Probation Officer, calm in the face of Charles' frantic promises, 'it is not going to be quite so easy. To start with, Gina could go to prison – though I shall do what I can to avoid this. There was clearly no criminal intent. But even if the Magistrate is lenient, he'll put her on probation and as you can probably appreciate, Mr Martin, a woman on probation would not be considered as a suitable adoptive parent.'

'But she's done all this because she wants a child so much!' Charles protested. 'She hasn't committed a crime!'

'Yes, she has. No matter how she felt, what she did was a crime. And since we are facing a few facts, Mr Martin, I must point out to you that your wife isn't in an emotionally stable frame of mind at the moment. Nor are you. She needs medical attention; a psychiatrist to help her to bring what amounts to an obsession into a proper perspective. That is what I shall say to the Magistrate and that is what I hope very much he will agree to.'

'Then Gina won't be able to have a baby – even though I'm willing now that I know how she feels?'

'Not for a while. But eventually, there is no reason why not. Her probation will end and then you will both be free – to make a fresh start.'

'Will she be allowed to come home with me – if she is put on probation? Or will she go to a hospital?'

'I'm sure the Magistrate would agree, if it is to be probation, that she should be released in your care – provided he considers you a responsible person, and provided that your wife wants to go home with you. I'll send her in to talk it over with you, shall I? It would be best to have these kind of details ironed out before we go back into court.'

When Gina's case was resumed the Magistrate, acting as he so often did on the probation officer's report, put Gina on probation for one year and instructed Charles that she should have psychiatric treatment, for as long as was considered necessary by the doctor in charge.

They drove off in Charles' car.

12

Despite his relief that Gina had got off so lightly, Charles was desperately worried, worried because he could make no contact with Gina. She did not cry. She sat beside him in the car dry-eyed, mute, almost as if she were not there. He tried desperately to make conversation – to evoke some response but after a little while, his scraps of news about his work, Myra – even Linda, were exhausted and he, too, fell silent.

He felt a deep ache in his heart. What had happened to their marriage that they could sit one beside the other like this – strangers? Was it his fault? Or Gina's? Or both? Somehow he had failed her and yet although he was willing now, for *her* sake, to adopt a child, he felt that it might, after all, be too late for his change of heart.

He still experienced a sickening sense of shock at what had happened. That Gina – his lovely, gay, vivacious Gina – should have been reduced to stealing some other woman's child! It was horrible and yet now suddenly, it made sense. She had wanted a baby so much. If only she had confided in him – told him how desperate she was!

Surely she must have known that he would give way rather than let her do something like this.

But there had been no confidences from Gina – no contact between them for months – not since her illness. She had shut herself away from him – shut him out from her thought; kept him at arm's length emotionally as well as physically. For all he knew, she had stopped loving him.

He drove faster – hating the trend of his thoughts; hating the invisible barrier which kept him from pouring questions at the girl sitting so silently beside him and forcing her to answer.

They were home. Automatically, Gina went to the kitchen and put on the kettle. She felt numb – like a zombie who had neither will nor reason. Not even Charles' desperate efforts to be normal and conversational could stir her from this blessed feeling of *not* feeling anything at all.

'Tired, darling?' Charles was asking solicitously.

She nodded. Yes, she was tired – tired of fighting, tired of hoping, tired of everything.

'I'm going to put you to bed and ask Dr Williams to come and give you something to make you sleep!'

She did not argue. Charles could do as he pleased. What he did no longer concerned her.

Charles undressed her as if she were a child; put her between the sheets and gave her a hot water bottle for her icy feet. Then he phoned the doctor.

'Shock!' said the doctor when he came down from Gina's room to join Charles in the sitting room. 'She'll get over it and then you'll be able to get her to talk about it. Most unfortunate – but I'm not altogether surprised. I would say that frustration of the maternal instinct is probably one of the most effective of nerve destroyers.'

'But she'll get better? Get over it?'

Charles' voice was taut with anxiety.

'With care, yes! I think it is a splendid idea that she should see a psychiatrist – it's the mind we're dealing with now rather than a physical ill and that's outside my province.'

Charles was suddenly angry.

'If you knew this might happen, why didn't you do something about it? Maybe this dreadful thing could have been avoided.'

The doctor was patient.

'You cannot force people to go to their doctors and take a prescribed cure. If Gina had wanted my help or advice, she could have come to me. I did prescribe tranquillizers for her after she was so ill – and I told her to come back for another prescription if she didn't feel better.'

'She didn't come!'

'No! You have to try and see this from her

186

point of view. Why should she? She's an intelligent girl. She knew I was offering her a sedative when what she still needed was a baby. A tranquillizer must have seemed a pretty poor substitute, don't you think?'

Charles sighed.

'I'm not trying to pass the blame on to you, Doctor. I know that somewhere along the line, I'm to blame. I'm her husband and it was up to me to see that she was happy. I truly believed she'd get over this Linda affair and return to her normal self. We used to be so happy together...' He broke off to stare into the fire which was just beginning to burn brightly with a cheerful crackling and spitting of the logs. The sound brought back a memory, painful and acute, of how they had once made love here in front of the fire...

'You mustn't get morbid about all this. It has happened before and no doubt it will happen again. But now you do know what your wife is feeling, it's up to you to try and help her as much as you can. Be gentle, loving – let her see what she means to you. Even if she doesn't respond, it does matter very much that she knows you care. Don't leave her alone any more than you can help ... and don't hesitate to call me in if you think she's in need of me.'

Later that evening Gina woke to find Myra at her bedside. For a moment, she was unsure where she was. She had dreamed she was still in the hotel – trying to get Michael to sleep and knowing that she would be late laying the tables for supper. Involuntarily, she glanced round the room for Michael's cot and then she realized that she was home … that she would never see Michael again.

Tears, hot, stinging, filled her eyes. Seeing them Myra leant forward and grasped her hand.

'Don't, Gina! It's all over now, darling, and you're quite safe and we all love you. Please don't cry!'

Gina gave a long shuddering sob.

'I wish I could die!' she said, choking on the words. 'I wish I could die!'

Myra became suddenly the sensible elder sister. She said briskly:

'Snap out of it, Gina. It isn't like you to be a coward. What you did was very wrong – I wonder if you realize just how much worry you caused poor Charles – not to mention the wretched woman whose baby you took. But dying isn't going to make amends for what you did. You've got to live, darling, and however hard it may seem, you've got to make it up to Charles. He's been out of his mind with worry and misery.'

Gina was now crying silently. Her eyes were closed and the tears slid from between the lids and down her white cheeks. Pity for her stirred Myra's heart but she steeled herself against showing it.

'Charles loves you very, very much, Gina. I don't know if you realize what you mean to him. Once upon a time I thought you loved him, too. Remember the day you met – at my wedding? That night, you told me afterwards, you grew up and fell in love. It can't have all gone. Charles has done nothing to forfeit that love. It wasn't *his* fault you couldn't have a child. I know you blame him for not letting you keep Linda – but try and see it from his point of view. He didn't love Linda the way you did. It would have been dishonest and wrong, Gina, quite, quite wrong for Linda, if Charles had agreed to adopt her. Children sense these things even if Charles had managed not to show how he felt. He just did not love her.'

Gina was no longer crying. Her eyes were still shut but Myra knew she was listening.

'Try to be fair about all this, Gina. What you've just done was a terrible thing for everyone – including yourself. Don't you realize it could never work? Charles told me about that hotel where you were working. What kind of life would that have been for the baby when he began to grow up? And what kind of life for you? When you'd grown used to having the child, you would have started to remember Charles again – remember what it was like to have a man to look after you; love you. You'd have wanted him back, Gina – and you'd have lost him.'

'It would have been enough – having the baby!'

'No, Gina. You don't know what you are talking about. I've had children and I love them dearly but children aren't meant to be all of a woman's life. A woman needs a man and you would have wanted Charles, as a companion, as a protector, as a lover, as a husband. You need to grow up, Gina. Life isn't a game – the kind of game you used to play with Mark. Mark spoilt you – let you grow up believing you could have everything in the world you wanted. But no one can have everything, and you are luckier than hundreds of other lonely wretched women who never know what it is to love and be loved. It makes me angry to hear you saying you wish you were dead when you have a husband like Charles to live for.'

Gina did not reply. Myra left her and not long after, Charles came in with her supper on a tray.

'I'm … not … very hungry…'

'I know. But please try and eat something. Dr Williams says you are far too thin. He's given me a prescription for an iron tonic and vitamins and entrusted me to see that you take them.'

He put the tray down and propped up the pillows behind her head. For such a large, strong man, his movements were extraordinarily tender and careful. Gina looked at him and a small part of the iron band round her heart eased its pressure, leaving her vulnerable. She felt again – not love but regret for having hurt this man who loved her. She said:

'I'm sorry!'

The childish words brought him a moment of acute pain. To cover his feelings, he said quickly:

'We won't talk about it – not unless you want to.'

She bit her lip.

'I – I'd like to talk about it – but I can't – not just yet. Perhaps – in a little while…'

'Of course. Now eat something, Gina. Myra cooked it so it should be nice.'

He sat with her until she fell asleep. Then he went downstairs and telephoned his foreman to say he was taking a fortnight's holiday to look after his wife. It was a busy time for him and he knew he might lose some valuable contracts – but he didn't care. Nothing in the world could make him leave Gina now until he was assured of her recovery.

It was not easy for him. During the next few days Gina resumed her everyday life in the cottage, but she was always quiet. He never once saw her smile. She accepted his many attentions passively, gratefully, but he knew that she could not return his love.

When he held her hand, she would not draw it away but it was like holding the hand of someone asleep; there was no answering pressure. When he kissed her good night, she returned his kiss like a child – never like a woman quickening with warmth and passion and hunger.

It was almost a relief when the day came to take her to the hospital for her first visit to the psychiatrist. Nothing he had been able to do since she had come home had seemed to make her want to live – to bring her fully alive. Maybe the doctors could help.

But her first visit, about which she told him nothing, made little difference that Charles could see. She cooked, cleaned the cottage, helped him a little in the garden, went for drives or to the cinema – outwardly co-operative and yet always without that will of her own. He would have welcomed an argument – a disagreement – anything to prove that she felt something...

At the end of the fortnight, he went back to work. He would have taken longer but Gina expressed no desire for him to stay. If she had clung to him and begged him not to leave her, wild horses would not have dragged him away.

When he came home at night she always had supper ready, a fire lit and she had changed her clothes, made up her face. Each night he asked himself with a desperate hope if she had done this to please him – to attract him. But she remained remote, withdrawn and it was obviously an effort for her to make conversation and appear to be pleased to have him home.

The weeks went by. There were regular visits to the hospital – to the Probation Officer – to the family doctor. Gina began to put on a little weight and to regain some colour. Then came the invitation to Mark's and Ilse's wedding. For two days Charles hid the card from Gina – wondering if this would in some way upset her. Finally, he showed it to her and said:

'Mark has asked me to be best man. What do you think, darling?'

'Of course, if you'd like to be!'

Myra's children and Linda were to be bridesmaids and page. Charles insisted that Gina buy something new to wear for the wedding. He hoped that this might rouse some enthusiasm. She showed him the two-piece suit she had chosen but there was no excitement accompanying her unpacking of the dress-box. He tried not to show his disappointment.

'It's lovely, darling!' he said, and gave her money to buy a hat and shoes to go with it.

A week before the wedding, Charles was asked to see the psychiatrist at the hospital – without Gina present. What the man said to him filled him with a new, incredible belief in himself, in life, in the future.

'Your wife is quite normal in herself now. She has this whole business in its proper perspective and if not yet resigned to the fact that she can't have children, she accepts that it is the misfortune of some people not to have everything they want in life.'

'But she is not normal – at least, she is not her old self. We – we don't quarrel or anything but she is entirely passive, she keeps me at arm's length. I may be her friend but never her lover.'

The man smiled.

'That's because she feels so guilty – she knows that she must have hurt you terribly by her actions and yet you have never reproached her; never stopped loving her. She told me that. She feels now that she isn't worthy of your love and that before she can accept it she must find some way to atone for what she did.'

'But that isn't necessary. Oh, I was hurt – bitterly hurt. I was jealous, too, but I understand that she wasn't really in her right mind when she did those things. Doesn't she realize that all I want is to have her back – to be as we used to be before all this?'

'I think she does realize it – but she can't find a way to pull down the barrier she put up between you. She told me you share a double bed, but that you sleep as far apart as possible – that this was of her choosing. But she can't make herself cross that barrier. That's why I have asked to see you – it's up to you now, Mr Martin, to help her.'

'She knows I've come to see you today. Whatever I do now, she will imagine it is because you told me to.'

'A very astute young man. I see I can leave everything in your hands quite safely. She's a lucky young woman – to have a husband as much in love with her as you are. There's just one more thing,' said the doctor as Charles rose to go. 'It's about that inability of hers to have children. I've been making some enquiries and I'm told that there are some entirely new techniques for dealing with a case like your wife's. It is just possible that a series of operations might put right the fault. You've probably read in the papers about the new successes with grafting spare parts.'

Charles stared back at the man incredulously.

'You've told this to Gina?'

'No! There are two reasons – first that my job has been to restore her to a balanced state of mind. I think I have succeeded in making her see that her life can be, if she chooses to make it, a happy one in its relationship with you. Then I wanted to see how you would feel about this whole experiment – for that is what it would mean.

Series of operations and possibly at the end of them, failure. They could even be dangerous – for your wife.'

Charles remained silent.

'Endanger her life?'

'It is possible, yes! I think your wife would agree to take these risks because she knows that you cannot love a child which is not your own. For her part, I hardly need to tell you, she would be quite happy to adopt a baby. I think the choice of action is really up to you.'

Charles sat down again. This news was totally unexpected. A possible cure for whatever it was that prevented Gina from having children – possible, but dangerous, experimental.

'I wouldn't consider it – not if it was dangerous for Gina.'

'I thought you might say that. At the same time, you have to see this from your wife's point of view. She is a highly maternal person. Even as a very small girl, she wanted children. When she married you, it wasn't just because she wanted you for her lover; she chose you as a father to her children as well; as head of the house; the protector, provider.'

'I know that. But I can't let her risk her *life* – and for what – to produce my child! No, doctor, I would far prefer that she adopt a baby. I want her to be happy – to have what she wants.'

He had said it before to the Probation Officer at the court, but it had not been true then. All he had wanted then was to get Gina back – it was a means to an end, nothing more. Now, quite suddenly, he knew that he didn't mind. He just wanted her to be happy – to hear her laugh again...

He remembered suddenly the days of their engagement when he had watched her with Myra's baby. She had been so gentle and patient and it had filled his heart with a special extra quality of love to realize that this glowing, vital tempestuous girl was all woman; that she could be this way with children as well as be the ardent passionate girl he would hold in his arms. If she had not been capable of loving and wanting children, she would not have been his Gina.

'No!' he said aloud but to himself rather than to the man opposite him. 'No, I really *want* her to adopt a child.'

At first, Gina put the tension she seemed to feel in the air down to the wedding. Everyone was rushing around excited and happy. Ilse was being married from Myra's house and they were all crowded into the bungalow getting in each other's way.

Gina was helping to dress the children. Betsy-Ann and Linda looked angelic in their tiny white and blue polka-dot muslin dresses. Robert looked equally cherubic in blue velvet trousers and white frilled nylon shirt. Upstairs Myra was helping Ilse into her wedding gown. In the dining room Malcolm, Mark and Charles, in morning dress, were calming their nerves with the aid of a bottle.

Through the open door, Gina could hear Charles' voice. It was deeper-toned than Malcolm's or Mark's but she could not hear what he was saying. She fixed Betsy-Ann's tiny floral coronet and simultaneously, heard Charles laugh. Something turned over inside her. She had not heard him laugh in so long.

The men came through into the room, talking and admiring the children's appearance. Kneeling beside Robert, Gina looked up and saw Charles' eyes staring at her. He wasn't laughing now. His look was searching, penetrating, unwavering. She felt the colour rush to her cheeks and she turned away quickly.

Then the cars came. Gina and Myra went with the children. Then Mark with Charles. Finally Malcolm, who was giving away the bride, with Ilse, pale but smiling, on his arm.

Gina went into the front pew beside her sister. In front of the altar, Charles stood beside Mark, taller, broader and upright. She thought suddenly of her wedding day when Charles had worn these same clothes and had stood waiting for her as she walked up the aisle towards him – so tall, so straight, so handsome...

The organ began to play and heads turned to watch the bride enter the church. Charles, too, had turned but he was not looking at Ilse – he was staring at her. She looked back at him and felt her legs tremble – just as they had trembled when she walked that long length of the aisle towards him. It was as if it were she, not Ilse, who was the bride, moving nearer until they were hand in hand...

She closed her eyes quickly and when she opened them, Charles had his back towards her and the ceremony had begun. She could not follow the words. Her eyes were on Charles' back, bewildered and yet riveted there. Her heart was beating furiously. She had a feeling of panic and then of emptiness.

She felt Myra's arm on hers – heard her sister's voice, whispered, anxious:

'You all right, Gina?'

She nodded. Then it was suddenly all over – the bride and groom, smiling at each other, arms tightly linked, were coming down the aisle from the vestry. Ilse looked radiant – Mark happy and confident. The children walked behind them, solemn, serious round eyes and little foreheads creased in concentration. The organ was filling the church with music. Gina closed her eyes and felt an arm touch hers.

'Gina?' His hand closed over hers, holding it tightly, painfully tightly, in his own. He led her down the aisle out into the sunshine. Photographs were being taken – the black shining cars with their gay white ribbons were moving slowly towards the door. The bride and groom climbed into the first car – the children with their parents followed and then Charles was sitting beside her in the next car.

He was smiling down at her.

'Not quite the correct protocol!' he said. 'But I suddenly wanted my wife to myself.'

His hand was still holding hers, their fingers interlinked and gripping fiercely. Gina was trembling.

'You look so very lovely!'

They were the same words he had spoken after their own wedding on the way from the church to the reception. He, too, must be remembering, Gina thought.

How happy she had been – how afraid that she might fail him, how filled with an almost sacred desire to make her husband a good wife – the happiest man in the world. How much she had loved him – how eager to prove she would never fail him!

The car stopped at the hotel where the reception was to be held. They were shown into the large room where the bride and groom stood waiting to receive their guests. The wedding cake was on the spotless white-clothed table. Charles let go her hand and took up his place beside Mark. The guests began to arrive and the room slowly filled with people.

For Gina, the wedding party was lived in a kind of dream. She talked with the guests, kissed Ilse, kissed Mark with a real affection, as she wished him every happiness. She fixed Betsy-Ann's coronet and took Robert off to wash his hands. But all the time she was barely conscious of her actions, for wherever she moved, whatever she did, she was always conscious of Charles somewhere in the room, watching her. Again and again their eyes met but he did not come near her. He stood with a crowd of people between them and yet it was as if they were the only two people in the room.

The hours passed. Ilse and Mark went to change, came down and were waved off with a shower of forbidden confetti and a lot of laughter. And there was Charles, beside her, saying:

'Shall we go now?'

They slipped away unnoticed. Charles had his own car now and she sat beside him, looking at his hands, strong and brown, on the steering wheel. After a while she noticed that they were not going home.

'Where are we going?'

'You'll see!'

They were the only words they spoke until they drew up outside a road house. Then Charles pulled in to the car park and switched off the ignition, and said:

'Remember?'

Gina remembered. How could she forget this place – the place where they had all come after Myra's wedding; the place where she had danced the night away and known that she was in love – in love with Charles.

They had drinks in the bar. Charles was very gay – talking to the men who ribbed him about his morning dress and asking why wasn't his bride all in white. Then they dined, Charles carrying all the conversation, discussing the wedding, the guests, Gina barely listening to his words for he was saying something else to her at the same time with his eyes...

They danced. It was a long, long time since they had danced. Charles requested numbers from the bandleader – tunes they had danced to the night they fell in love. Charles' arm tightened round her, drawing her closer. His mouth was against her hair. She could feel his heart beating fiercely – but not as fiercely as her own.

Their evening followed the pattern of that first evening. Gina realized that Charles had organized just this – and was glad. It was as if the years between had been swept clean like a tide over an untidy beach. Now nothing mattered any more except that she had fallen in love again – with the same man. She had lost him but now they had found each other again.

The band played 'Goodnight, Sweetheart'. Charles silently paid the bill and led her out to the car. As on that first night, he took her in his arms and kissed her.

Now at last she was really alive – lifting her face and returning his kisses with the same shy ardour that there had been before. He was a stranger, and yet not a stranger. She had known him and loved him all her life.

He drove home very slowly because he was steering with one hand. The other lay entwined with hers as if he could not bear to be without this physical contact. She waited silent and breathless while he put the car in the garage and then he was lifting her in his arms and the dream changed from that first night to their wedding night.

He carried her upstairs and undressed her. He did not kiss her but laid her down on the bed. She waited for him to undress. The room was in darkness but as he moved in beside her, he reached up and switched on the light. Their eyes met and he smiled.

Something in Gina that had been slowly thawing throughout the day, melted into a glowing warmth. The dreadful feeling of isolation from other human beings and from Charles in particular, was quite suddenly gone. As she held out her arms to him, she was conscious of an actual physical transformation and if Charles had asked her to explain, she would have told him that the iron bands that were encasing her had become like gossamer threads which he alone could break.

'I love you!' she whispered and the words spoken with a glorious freedom from pain were more true than they had ever been before.

'Gina, my love, my love!'

There was pain as well as joy in his voice and she knew an answering pain in her heart. How terribly she had hurt him! And how little he had deserved that cold rejection. It had never been his fault that, being a man, he had failed to appreciate how desperately she wanted a baby. Because she had completely fulfilled his life, he had believed that so he could fulfil hers. She would never again let him believe that buried in her heart was the same longing for a child to complete their family circle. She would hide that unfulfilled part of her nature and spend her life in making him happy.

'I've been such a fool!' she said softly. 'I was angry because you would not let me have what I wanted. I don't mind any more – not now that we are together again. You are all I want, Charles – all that I need.'

He believed her – or at least believed that she meant what she said. Her words filled his heart with a great singing joy. He need never again feel that he was unimportant to her – that her need of him came second to that of her need for a child.

Then strangely, with the knowledge that he came first, his opposition to her adopting a child vanished. He had told the psychiatrist that he would agree to Gina adopting a baby but it had been for her sake – not because he, himself, had wanted one. Now, strangely, he did. He did not understand why he should feel this way but it was part of the closeness to Gina – as if they were thinking now as one person and that despite her words, her innermost dreams had been transmitted to him.

Presently he would try to tell her how he felt. But now she was not needing words from him. Her beautiful grey eyes were speaking their own words, telling him that he was wanted, needed and loved. With a new wisdom born of his new maturity, he was aware that this was their real wedding night – the moment when they were united in their spiritual as well as their physical desires.

Their joy in one another was never so complete.

13

Twelve years later

The two girls sat side by side on the locker, their backs against the radiator, their arms clasped round hunched knees.

'Only another week before the hols!' said the younger girl, Charlotte, her voice trembling a little with excitement.

Her friend, a plump thirteen-year-old called Susan, stared at her companion curiously.

'You live in Sussex, don't you? That can't be so far from here. Couldn't you have been a day-girl?'

Charlotte's face clouded, the excitement in her shining brown eyes ebbing into a withdrawn blankness. After a minute, she said slowly:

'Yes, I suppose I could!'

Susan put an arm round her friend and gave her an unselfconscious hug. She was a demonstrative, affectionate girl and Charlotte's opposite in every way. The other girls thought it amusing that these two should have become close friends. Charlotte was thin, tall, leggy and rather quiet. Susan was round, plump, friendly and noisy. They complimented one another and their friendship was important to them both. Charlotte was in her second term at the school, Susan had been there a year. Last term, although the two girls had noticed one another, neither had made the first overtures of friendship. It was not until they found each other in the same dormitory this term that a close friendship had really developed.

Although Susan was the elder by nearly a year, already Charlotte was the leader of the two. Susan, in her easy affectionate way, was quite happy to do whatever Charlotte wanted. She adored her friend with schoolgirlish intenseness and was sometimes a little hurt because Charlotte could not respond in the same demonstrative way. However, a term had been sufficient to realize that Charlotte's friendship was none the less sincere because it was not so obvious and now she was no longer hurt when a hug was not returned.

'You never talk much about your home!' Susan said. 'You're an only child, aren't you? Do you think that's why you were sent to boarding school?'

Unknowingly Susan had opened a wound which still hurt so fiercely that Charlotte had never allowed herself to think about the reasons for being at school. Tears pricked behind her eyes and she quickly drew out a handkerchief and said:

'My cold seems to be getting worse!'

The two girls had been excused lacrosse this cold grey December day because of their colds and were enjoying the unusual and welcome privacy of an empty classroom in which to pass the afternoon.

Outside the window, the dark clouds of approaching rain were scurrying across a damp grey sky. From the playing fields an occasional shout would carry across the lawns just audible in the classroom. In half an hour it would be dark and the other girls would come bursting in one by one, and the smell of school soap and fresh air would temporarily overcome the normal smell of ink and chalk and desks.

Suddenly, to Susan's surprise and pleasure, Charlotte said:

'I'll tell you a secret – if you swear on the Bible you'll never tell another living soul.'

'Of course, I won't tell. You know I'd never give away your secrets, Charlotte!'

'All the same, will you swear – on the Bible?'

Charlotte walked, with her usual unhurried grace, over to her desk and pulled out a Bible. Silently she handed it to her friend. Susan, her plump freckled face frowning in the seriousness of the moment, swore a sacred oath.

'Well, what is the secret?'

'I'm adopted. You didn't know, did you?'

'Golly, no, I didn't! You mean, your mother and father aren't your *real* mother and father?'

Charlotte was momentarily happy at the effect this news had on her friend. At the same time, she half regretted that the secret was out. Somehow, to talk about it made it more real.

She sat down again beside her friend and suddenly felt a desire to talk. She had never talked about it to anyone before.

'I was only a tiny baby when my parents adopted me, so of course, I never knew my real parents.'

Susan looked at her friend sympathetically. The information she had been given only increased her interest in and affection for Charlotte.

'I'd never have *known!*' she commented. 'You look just like that picture of your mother.'

'We are a bit alike, only of course, I'll never be as pretty!'

She felt a sudden pain remembering her father's words to her mother:

'I'll admit there is a likeness but she'll never be as lovely as you, my darling!'

They hadn't known she could hear. She had cried with bitter disappointment. She had copied her mother's hair style and tried to imitate her movements and expressions –

not just because she adored her mother with an almost painful adoration and love, but because she had so much wanted her father's admiration and love, too.

She had tried not to feel jealous of her mother but secretly she longed to be loved as her father loved her mother. No one else really mattered to him but Mummy. He was fond of his daughter and never unkind or unjust to her, but to the growing girl, it had become painfully obvious these last two years that she could never hope to compete with her mother.

Charlotte thought her father very handsome. He was, she told her friend now, everything a man should be – tall and strong and full of fun. She would have given her right arm *and* her place in the lacrosse team to know that her father loved her as much as he loved her mother. She constantly sought his approval and prayed at night that she would grow to be beautiful so that he would pay her the same marvellous compliments he was always paying Mother.

Susan was chattering on about the adoption, finding it exciting and mysterious. But it was not like this to Charlotte. She felt deep in her bones that it was the nameless 'thing' which lay between her and her father. If she had really been born to them, he would have loved his daughter more. She never had this feeling with her mother. Mother and she were so close it was impossible to imagine being closer.

They had wonderful times together – especially lately now that she was growing up. They went shopping together – choosing clothes or new curtains; going to the cinema on wet afternoons and hurrying back on the top of the bus to get the fire lit and Daddy's supper cooked before he came home.

They spent many hours together poring over recipe books in the kitchen; trying out new dishes they thought Daddy might enjoy or preparing the more complicated ones if they knew they were his favourites. At weekends, it was not quite so perfect. Daddy liked to have Mummy to himself and although he never meant to make Charlotte feel an unwelcome third, she always felt *de trop.*

Mummy hadn't wanted her to go to boarding school. It had been Daddy's idea.

'It isn't good for her to be so much with grown-ups,' he had said. 'She needs the company of other children. She's twelve years old and to talk to her sometimes, you'd think she was eighteen!'

In the end Mummy had agreed. She always, in the end, did what Daddy wanted. But again, intuition told Charlotte that it wasn't so much for *her* sake that she was being sent away to school, but because Daddy would have more of Mummy's time and attention.

Strangely, it didn't make her dislike her father. She would have argued fiercely against any such idea. No one could dislike her father. It wasn't as if he were a bad father – he was never unkind, over-severe – unjust. He wouldn't, for instance, send her up to bed before her nine o'clock bedtime but she knew that when her bedtime came, he would somehow be happier because he would be alone with Mummy. Now he'd have all the term to be alone with Mummy. In a way, it had made a difference last holidays – Daddy had seemed very pleased to have her home and he hadn't been nearly so strict about bedtime. It was as if he realized that she would only be there for a short while and that he could afford to include her in that electric, magic circle of love he put round Mummy.

The holiday had been great fun. Uncle Mark had come to stay with his three little boys, all fair haired and blue-eyed like Aunt Ilse. There'd been another family party with Uncle Malcolm and Aunt Myra and the children. Her cousins. Betsy-Ann was fifteen now and rather inclined to be bossy; but Robert, who was seventeen and almost a man, was a little bit in love with her and this did a lot to restore her morale even if her heart was quite untouched by the rather spotty gangling tongue-tied youth.

Most of all, Charlotte liked Linda. Linda, too, was adopted and both girls felt a special link between them because of this. Linda was seventeen, a thin, pale girl who kept very much in the background so that one was apt not to notice her. She was engaged to be married to a solicitor's clerk and wore a diamond engagement ring of which she was very proud. Charlotte had heard her mother and Aunt Myra discussing him.

'He's quiet, like Linda!' Aunt Myra had said. 'He isn't all that brainy but he adores Linda and she seems to think he's perfect. Incredible, isn't it, to think that only the other day she was a tiny scrap of a thing you rescued from that Home. It's fifteen years and it seems like last week!'

Later, Charlotte had asked Mummy about the Home where Linda had come from and Mummy had told her how she had nearly adopted Linda but that she had become ill and Aunt Myra had adopted her instead.

'I'm very glad, too!' Mummy had said. 'If I'd had Linda I might not have had you and that doesn't bear thinking about.'

Uncle Mark was nice – Charlotte liked him better than Uncle Malcolm. Daddy didn't seem to like him much and always made a bit of a fuss when he was due to come on a visit. She'd asked Mummy why Daddy didn't like him after their last visit and Mummy had laughed and said:

'Oh, well, I suppose Daddy is a bit jealous. Uncle Mark knew me long before Daddy did

213

and we were childhood sweethearts. Daddy can't forget I *might* have married Uncle Mark.'

'I'm glad you didn't. I like Daddy best!'

'So do I!' Mummy had said, hugging her.

Life, thought Charlotte, as she pressed her back against the radiator, was very exciting. As you grew up you discovered all sorts of things about grown-ups that you never thought of as a child. When you were little, it was things which mattered – a doll's broken arm or a trip to the circus, or doughnuts for tea! As you got older, it was people who mattered and how you felt about them and how they felt about you. She was suddenly no longer sorry she had told Susan her secret. It made their friendship closer and it was good to have friends. Ever since she had been sent away to boarding school, she had been a bit depressed. Silly though it was, she could not quite forget the feeling of rejection – of Daddy not wanting her at home; in some strange way, having Susan to love and admire her and think she was beautiful and exciting, made up for a lot. It was the same kind of feeling she had knowing Robert thought she was marvellous.

'Do you realize,' Susan was saying breathlessly, 'that for all you know, you might be a princess. I think it's frightfully exciting, you being adopted.'

Charlotte relaxed, able suddenly to see

herself through her friend's eyes. They spent a completely satisfying five minutes imagining all the romantic origins Charlotte might have had.

'Even your name is unusual!' Susan said.

Charlotte laughed.

'Well, there's nothing mysterious about that. I'm called after my father – his name is Charles. When I'm married, if I have a boy, I shall call him Charles. It's my favourite name. I don't like Charlotte much.'

They spent another five minutes thinking up names for the children they might one day have. The names became more and more ridiculous and before long both girls were doubled up with laughter.

'Antimacassar!' shrieked Susan.

'Pennycillin!' said Charlotte. 'Do you know, I once had a doll called Pennycillin – it was ages before I found out it was the name of a drug. I loved that doll. My mother said she had a doll like that once – called Lucy. She was always playing with dolls – much more than I used to. I like doing things with my hands. I wish I'd been a boy and could be an engineer. D'you know, Susan, I'd love to be able to work in my father's wrought-iron business. Maybe I will one day – I'm quite good at drawing and Mummy says I could perhaps design things for him. I don't want to get married too soon – I'd really enjoy working with Daddy. I'll tell you another secret – I'm doing a whole book of sketches for him for Christmas – would you like to see them?'

She went to her locker and took out a drawing book. Susan looked through it with gasps of admiration.

'Why, they're lovely, Charlotte! Look at that gate – it's like lace! And I think that little curvy balcony is perfectly adorable. Golly, you are clever, Charlotte! I should think your father will be ever so pleased!'

'Do you really?' Charlotte's face flushed with pleasure. 'I'm keeping it as a surprise – even Mummy doesn't know. Gosh, I wish Christmas would hurry up – three more weeks. I can't wait!'

'Nor me!' agreed Susan.

But somehow the time did rush by. There were end of term exams, the school play in which both girls had quite large parts; then clearing up the classroom and packing trunks. The last half-hour was somehow the hardest part of waiting. Then the cars began to roll up the drive and there was the old Morris with Daddy as well as Mummy come to collect her.

Charlotte's face was pink with pleasure as she scrambled into the back seat.

'It's marvellous you could come, Daddy. I never thought you would as it's Wednesday.'

'I decided to take a day off. You look well, Charlotte!'

'Keep your eyes on the road!' Mummy said laughing.

'You're just jealous because you have such a pretty daughter!'

Charlotte sank back happily into the worn old leather seat. Of course, Daddy wasn't serious – she and Mummy both knew he thought Mummy prettier, but it was nice all the same to hear Daddy teasing her.

They plied her with questions about school; told her some of the plans for the holidays. There was to be a big family gathering on Boxing Day – Aunt Myra and all her family, including Linda's fiancé; Uncle Mark and his family.

'That'll be fourteen of us!' Mummy said. 'I think it will be great fun.'

'I still don't see why Mark's crowd has to be there – they aren't family!'

'Oh, Charles, they are in a way – Myra and I have known Mark ever since we can remember. Besides, it's nice for Charlotte to have his children to play with. Myra's children are all older.'

'Okay, okay! I've said already I won't raise any objections. Now, Charlotte, what do you want to do for Christmas?'

Charlotte smiled. It was wonderful to be back with them – wonderful to listen to them – the two people whom she loved best in the world; wonderful beyond price to know that they were glad to have her home.

14

Charlotte was happy – so happy that she didn't want to talk. She sat drowsily staring round the drawing room, listening to the murmurs of conversation, wondering why one should feel like crying when one was so perfectly and wonderfully content.

It was a fabulous Christmas. Everyone, grown-ups and children, had seemed to conspire together to make this family gathering quite perfect. It couldn't even spoil her contentment that Daddy had taken Mother for a drive and never suggested she should go with them.

Uncle Mark and Uncle Malcolm were smoking cigars. They looked like Uncles puffing away and nodding to each other. Charlotte smiled. They, like she, had probably eaten too much turkey and plum pudding.

She felt in the pocket of her dress and touched the silver charm bracelet Uncle Mark had given her. She had always wanted a charm bracelet. She couldn't wait to wear it. Unfortunately, poor Robert had given her a bracelet, too – not nearly so expensive – made of tortoise-shell. She'd thanked him warmly and slipped it on her wrist and when she had opened Uncle Mark's present, she hadn't the heart to hurt Robert's feelings by changing them over. And that had made Robert happy. Aunt Myra had given her a lovely frilly stiff petticoat – quite useless for school but all the more fun for that. A funny sort of present for Aunt Myra to give – she was usually so practical!

Aunt Ilse had given her a pretty little glass ornament from Sweden. When she got home she would put it on the shelf with all the other ornaments she had collected since she was little. Uncle Malcolm had given her a book, a lovely illustrated book called *Art Designing*. She wondered if Mummy had told him about the sketch book. Charlotte had been unable to resist showing it to Mummy when she got back from school. She didn't mind if she had told Uncle Malcolm – it wasn't a secret any more.

She thought contentedly of Daddy's face when he had opened his present on Christmas morning. At first, he had looked surprised, then he had given her a very strange searching sort of glance – it was almost as if he was apologizing to her for something, and he had said:

'Why, thank you, darling. I never knew you were so clever or so interested in the old firm!'

And he had looked through the pages

again, more carefully and stopped at one page and said:

'I might be able to use that idea – not bad – no, not bad at all. Yes, I think we could use that on that window box job for the hotel…'

And Mummy had given her hand a secret squeeze under the eiderdown and Charlotte had tried not to look too proud.

Linda was playing Monopoly with Mark's children. Now and again one of the grown-ups would turn and tell them not to make so much noise, but in voices which meant they didn't really mind. Aunt Ilse had gone into the kitchen to put the kettle on. When Mummy and Daddy came back they would have tea with buttered crumpets and Christmas cake.

Life was wonderful! Charlotte thought. School seemed a long, long way off. She and Susan had exchanged cards and presents bought at Woolworths and later this holiday Charlotte was going up to Nottingham to stay with her friend for a few days. Now she wasn't so glad she had accepted the invitation – she was too happy here at home. She glanced down for the hundredth time at the watch on her wrist. Four-fifteen. It was marvellous to own such a beautiful watch. It was tiny and delicate and it had seventeen jewels inside. It was the most beautiful watch she had ever seen. On the back was inscribed in minute writing: *With love from Mummy and*

Daddy, Christmas, 1960.

Daddy had warned her to take care of it and Mummy had said for her that of course she would – she was getting a big girl now and was quite old enough to understand that the watch was valuable. It would have been valuable even if it had not cost so much money – because it was from the two people she loved most in the world.

Aunt Myra got up and switched on the lights. Charlotte was surprised then to see how dark it had got.

'Looks like we might have snow after all!' Uncle Mark said.

'Doubt it – too blinking cold!'

'Charles and Gina are taking their time. Where did they say they were going?'

'Just for a run. Charles said he wanted some fresh air after all that dinner. Isn't that the car now?'

Charlotte listened. The room was suddenly quiet as if the whole world had stopped to listen. She felt a sudden complete change of mood. A moment ago she had been perfectly, pricelessly happy. Now, suddenly, she was shivering with a strange, unaccountable fear.

'Tea's ready!'

Charlotte looked up at Ilse's smiling face and said sharply:

'We can't have tea yet – Mummy and Daddy aren't back!'

Aunt Myra said:

'Why, Charlotte!'

'I ... I'm sorry. I ... I didn't mean to be rude!'

'Well, maybe you're right. We'll give them another five minutes. They can't be much longer.'

Charlotte looked at her watch. Four-twenty. Her eyes went to the window as Ilse moved across the room to draw the curtains. It was quite dark now – black and forbidding.

'Time Charles replaced that old Morris!' It was Uncle Malcolm's voice. 'Don't know why he doesn't get the new Cortina – not as if he can't afford to.'

'Sentimental!' Uncle Mark was laughing. 'Charles is a sentimental chap, you know.'

Charlotte, momentarily diverted, thought:

'Yes, it's true. I never thought of it before!'

She remembered a hundred and one little things Daddy was sentimental about. There was the invitation to Uncle Mark's wedding – he still had it on his desk and whenever Mummy suggested he throw that faded old thing away, he would smile at her in a special way and say 'not on your Nelly!' and it always made Mummy laugh. Then there were the little rituals like putting on the outside light so Daddy could see his way up from the garage; and after dinner when Mummy always made him sit in the wing armchair by the fire where she brought him his coffee and his pipe and the evening paper. Saturday afternoons were reserved for car cleaning. After lunch Mummy would fill the red plastic bucket with soap and water and look out the chamois leather and window cleaning fluid and brush and pan and polishing cloths. Then, when Daddy had finished his pipe, he'd collect everything in the wheelbarrow and go down to the garage to his car. If it was warm and sunny, Mummy and she went with him.

Then there were his favourite dishes – the special ones reserved for special occasions. Steak-and-kidney pudding was his favourite of all. Once Mummy forgot it on his birthday and he was dreadfully disappointed. Mummy often teased him. Nowadays, she'd say, they could afford to have the car washed and polished at the garage, or to have a pheasant for dinner if they wanted and a maid to fetch and carry for him. But Daddy always said no to everything but the maid – Mummy could have a maid if she wanted. But Mummy didn't want one either – they were all much happier, she said, on their own.

Daddy was most of all sentimental about anniversaries. Every year he took Mummy to the same rather shabby road house. Charlotte often wondered why they didn't choose somewhere more exciting – go up to

London, perhaps, to a theatre and to a real night club. It wasn't even as if the road house was where they had met.

'We just like it there!' Mummy told her, so that was that. Once Mummy had said:

'It's a great mistake, Charlotte, to spend your life wanting things you haven't got. You can ruin your life doing just that. Daddy and I like things just the way they are and we don't want anything to be any different. It probably seems very stick-in-the-mud to you but once we nearly lost everything – everything we had and after that, we both realized that what we found again was too precious ever to risk losing it.'

Charlotte didn't altogether understand but somehow it wasn't really important. Her parents were happy and loved each other and they loved her, too. That was all that was really important.

The telephone rang. Uncle Malcolm said:

'Maybe they've had a breakdown.'

He got up to answer the phone. Charlotte jumped up too. With a great effort of will, she refrained from shouting:

'Don't answer it. Please don't answer it!'

But it was too late. Uncle Malcolm was saying:

'Good God! No, of course ... my dear chap ... yes, of course, I'll bring her round at once ... at once.'

He put down the receiver, his face white

and uneasy. Charlotte ran across the room and shook him by the jacket lapels.

'What's happened? What's wrong? What's *wrong*, Uncle?'

'My dear! I'm afraid ... you'll have to be brave, my dear...'

'What's *happened?*'

'It's your mother – accident ... not Charles' fault – the van hit them on the left hand side ... we've got to be quick, Charlotte. She's asking for you.'

Charlotte let out her breath. It was all right after all ... Mummy wasn't dead – only hurt. The colour came back into her cheeks and she ran into the hall for her coat.

'I'd better come, too!' Aunt Myra said, and followed her out to the car. Uncle Malcolm kept saying:

'We've got to hurry, must hurry!'

Charlotte thought he was silly to get so panicky. If Mother was in hospital, then she'd be there for some days, if she'd been hurt. There was no need for such a hurry.

Aunt Myra was holding her hand. She was crying. Charlotte felt impatient. Crying wouldn't help anyone.

The streets were fairly empty. They reached the hospital in ten minutes. As they got out of the car, Uncle Malcolm said:

'Pray God we aren't too late!'

'Too late for what?' Charlotte asked, thinking: 'Surely they aren't so strict about visiting hours that they won't allow me to see my own mother when she's hurt.'

No one answered her. They went up the steps and the antiseptic smell of the hospital greeted them as they paused at the reception desk.

Uncle Malcolm gave their names and again he said:

'I hope to God we're not too late?'

Then a nurse came towards them and said gently:

'Perhaps you'd like to come into the waiting room. Mr Martin is there…' She gave Charlotte a quick look and added: 'I'm afraid Mrs Martin died five minutes ago. Doctor will explain.'

'Died!' Charlotte thought. 'But Daddy wouldn't have *allowed* Mummy to die; he never allowed her to go anywhere without him.'

Then she realized that Daddy couldn't have stopped Mummy dying – he couldn't have prevented it – only the doctors could have done that and they had failed. They would put her in a coffin and take her away. Daddy wouldn't allow it – he'd want to go with her.

She looked at her aunt and said quietly:

'I want to see Daddy, *now!*'

But Charles, when they walked into the waiting room, didn't want to see her.

226

15

They were going home. Charlotte sat beside her father and was glad that it wasn't the same familiar car. This was a hired Vauxhall which they'd use till Daddy decided what new car to buy. If it had been the Morris, she would have felt she was sitting in Mummy's seat...

The last week at Aunt Myra's had been a kind of nightmare. Daddy must have thought so too, for suddenly this morning, he'd said at breakfast:

'I'm going home!'

Then Charlotte had said she was, too, and there had been quite a scene. Daddy and Aunt Myra had thought it would be better if she stayed with her cousins. Charlotte had argued patiently but with a quiet stubbornness:

'I shall go home and look after Daddy. I know how to do it. I'm quite old enough now. I can cook and do the housework and ... and I *want* to go.'

'I can get a woman in to see to things!' Her father hadn't looked at her. He hadn't spoken to her since the accident – he hadn't spoken to anyone.

Charlotte said firmly:

'Mummy would have *wanted* me to go with him.'

Everyone stopped talking and stared at her – even her father. Then he said quietly:

'All right – she can come.'

When she packed her things, Aunt Myra had given her a little talk.

'Charlotte, you're so young. I don't know how to say this. I know you love your father and that you want to help him but … well, this has been the most terrible blow to him. He … he loved your mother so much. I don't suppose you can understand quite how much. Going back to the cottage – to your home … it'll be very hard for him. For you, too, of course, but so much worse for him. There will be memories everywhere.'

She stopped to wipe her eyes. Aunt Myra had cried a lot but Charlotte only cried at night, in bed when she was alone. She cried then partly because she missed her mother so much; and partly because she knew Daddy's heart was broken. She thought perhaps hers might have broken, too, if it hadn't been for having Daddy to look after. Maybe they hadn't reached the hospital in time but if they had got there, she knew exactly what Mummy would have said to her. She would have said:

'Look after Daddy, darling. Look after him for me.'

There hadn't been a chance yet, to help Daddy. They didn't let her go to the funeral. All the grown-ups went and she stayed with Robert. But now – now at last, she could begin to help Daddy.

'Charlotte, he won't be very good company for you. He's bound to fret terribly for a time. I'm afraid … afraid he may neglect you a bit. I really think it might be better for you to stay here with us.'

'I'm going with Daddy!' Charlotte said.

They parked the car in the garage. Charlotte stumbled on the path but Daddy did not stop to help her. He walked past her carrying the suitcases and went into the house.

It was very cold. Charlotte took off her coat and hung it behind the kitchen door and collected sticks and paper and laid the fire. While it was kindling, she put the kettle on. Daddy was in his bedroom. He'd gone straight up there and hadn't come down.

The fire began to burn brightly and the room looked more cheerful. Charlotte glanced at her watch. Mid-afternoon. In a little while she must start to prepare some supper. She took the cookery book from the kitchen drawer and carried it into the sitting room and knelt by the fire, looking through recipes. Tonight there was cold chicken which Aunt Myra had packed up for her so there would only be vegetables to prepare.

That was easy. She, herself, wasn't very hungry but Daddy might be. A man, Mummy often said, needed a good square meal.

Tears sprang to her eyes. She was suddenly heartrendingly aware that she wouldn't hear Mummy talking ever again. She would never come through that door, smiling her beautiful smile, saying in that lovely low voice of hers:

'Hullo, darling. I've got a lovely surprise for you and Daddy tonight.'

She dashed the tears away angrily. Mummy hated it when she cried. Besides, there was a lot to do.

She kept busy and time passed. Her father still did not come down but Charlotte thought he might be sleeping. She left him till the last minute when the table was laid, the candles lit and the meal all ready to put on the table. She took a last look at everything and nodded her head. It was all as Mummy always did it – the way they had often done it together.

She went up and knocked on her father's door.

'Dinner's ready!' she called.

He did not reply.

She called him again and this time his voice came back muffled, angry:

'For God's sake go away.'

She took a step back and swallowed nervously. He *had* to come down – it was all ready and she'd taken so much trouble…

'Daddy, please come down. I've cooked everything properly – really I have. And the chips are the way you like them – small and crisp. Please, Daddy!'

There was no answer. Slowly, she went back down the stairs. She sat down at the dining table and tried not to cry. Aunt Myra had warned her – she ought to be prepared for this – she'd told Aunt Myra she was old enough. But how could she look after Daddy if he didn't want to be looked after. The tears fell faster.

'Don't sniff, Charlotte! Get a handkerchief!'

She looked up and through her tears she saw him standing in the doorway.

'Well, go on,' he said.

His face was haggard. His mouth was set in a tight line as if he had himself rigidly under a control he did not trust.

Charlotte brought in the soup. They both ate only a little and she took it away and brought in the chicken. They ate in silence. Neither was hungry… Charlotte was too tired and Charles too tightly controlled. He refused the cheese and got up from the table.

Charlotte went over to the window table and got out his pipe and tobacco pouch. She felt a moment of relief – he was sitting in his usual chair. She put the pipe on the table beside him and went out to collect the coffee. During the afternoon the paper boy had put the evening edition through the letter box. She took it in with the coffee. She hadn't forgotten a single part of the evening ritual.

Charles was staring into the fire. Charlotte watched him nervously. When he turned and found her staring at him, he said:

'Well, what's wrong?'

'Your coffee is getting cold – and you haven't lit your pipe!'

He gave her a sudden look of sheer anguish and said cruelly:

'You'll never be like her, you know, no matter how hard you try!'

Charlotte stared at him, some faint glimmer of dormant feminine intuition telling her that he didn't mean it – he didn't mean to hurt her. It was just that he was so hurt himself.

She said:

'I know! If I'd really been born to her, it would be different. Then I'd really look like her and you'd sort of feel you still had a part of her left. It – it isn't so bad for me. You see, I've still got you.'

Her father was staring at her now, really looking at her.

'Me?'

'Why, yes! I loved you and Mummy the same amount so even though she's gone,

I've still got you to love, haven't I? But you haven't got anything but me!'

'Oh, Charlotte!' He put out an arm and pulled her towards him so that she stood between his knees, his head against her hair. 'You're a strange child – only a child – but you seem to understand. I … I've always been fond of you, you know. It's just that…'

'That you loved Mummy more. I know. I don't mind. If I'd been you, I'd have loved her more, too.'

'I nearly lost her once … before you were born. I never thought it could happen again … like this. Life doesn't seem to have any meaning now she has gone.'

'I know!' Charlotte said gravely. 'But Susan says you get used to it in time.'

'Susan?'

'My friend at school. Her mother ran away and left them and her father divorced her after a while and they never see her now. Susan says it was two years ago and they don't think of her very often any more.'

'She's a child!' Charles said, releasing her.

Charlotte curled up on the carpet and leant her cheek against his knee.

'Children can love people very much. I love Mummy so much I would die in her place if I could. I wish I had and I dare say you do, too.'

Charles touched her hair quickly and said: 'You mustn't ever think like that. You're young – you've got your whole life ahead of you.'

'Yes, I know. I mean to try very hard, Daddy – to look after you properly – the way Mummy wanted. I know I'm only twelve but I'll be thirteen soon and I can leave boarding school and then I'll be here all the time to take care of you.'

'No! It isn't that I don't want you, Charlotte … but boarding school is best for you now that … now that…'

'All right!' Charlotte agreed quickly. 'But there'll be the holidays, won't there? We could do things – together … sort of keep each other company.'

'Yes. We've got each other. Now it's time to go to bed. I'm sorry about the dinner… I'm just not awfully hungry.'

'No, nor was I!'

They looked at each other and briefly, Charles smiled. Then she stood up and kissed him and went up to bed.

For a long time he sat staring into the fire. After Charlotte's movements upstairs had ceased, the silence became complete. He wasn't sure how long he could stand it. His loss was too much to bear. The child meant well but she couldn't understand … no one could understand how destitute and desolate he felt. Never to see her again, to hold her hand, watch that radiant smile come into her eyes; never to hear her voice, her footsteps; never to feel her warm, soft body alight with a physical passion they had never lost through the years. How could a child understand this loss of the other part of himself?...

In three weeks' time it would have been their fifteenth wedding anniversary. He knew the date so well – and that other secret anniversary they kept each year, remembering the night of Mark's and Ilse's wedding – the night their true understanding of each other, their real marriage, had begun. It seemed such a little time ago now; only the other day that they had adopted Charlotte and Gina had said: 'This is the most precious of all your gifts to me, darling!' She had added: 'One day she'll be the most precious thing *I* can give *you*.' Why had she said that? He couldn't puzzle it out then and now it still did not make sense. In a way, Charlotte did matter to him very much. He was fond of her, proud of her, amused by her efforts to imitate her mother. Tonight those same efforts had at first angered him and then touched him. Poor little kid. It was a pity he'd never loved her – at least, not the way Gina did.

'The trouble with you, darling, is that you are so much love to me, there's none left over for poor Charlotte!'

When had Gina said that? The night he'd first suggested sending the child to boarding school. Perhaps it was true. While Gina lived, he hadn't wanted anything or anybody else. Yet somehow Gina had managed to love both of them. She had never given him cause to feel jealous of the child. Yet she had adored Charlotte. It was as if her heart had been loving enough to give fully to both of them. Why hadn't he managed to feel the same?

He asked himself now, for the first time in his life, if he had been a good father. The truth was that he had given the child everything that he could. It was not, as she had suggested tonight, that being an adopted child had made any difference. In a way, he was glad that she was not too like Gina to look at. That might have been more than he could bear, to see Charlotte a pale ghost of Gina – so nearly and yet never quite her. No, it was that he had not wanted anything to come between them, to touch that perfect love they shared.

And now that Gina was gone – the child was still in the way. But for her, he might have put an end to a life he no longer wanted. Upstairs in the bedroom, his grief and loneliness had been so terrible that he had been momentarily tempted to finish off his sufferings once and for all. It was Charlotte who had made it impossible. She had had one terrible enough shock – he couldn't give her such another.

A log collapsed into the fire and sent up a shower of sparks. Charles covered his face with his hands, tormented. It would be so much easier to die than to go on living; so much easier. Was this what Gina wanted – the hard way? Must he go on for the sake of her child?

'We could do things together – sort of keep each other company!' Charlotte's voice was wistful, pleading in his ear.

Well, maybe they could – or at least for a little while, until the child was grown up, married, didn't need him any more. Funny, grown-up little girl, cooking his meal, bringing his pipe and his paper the way she had seen her mother do...

'Oh, Gina, Gina!'

The silence became intolerable. He switched out the light and went upstairs. On the landing, he paused. Then, feeling a desperate desire for company, any company of any living being to help chase away the ghost of his lost love, he opened the door of Charlotte's room.

The child was sleeping. In her arms was a long-ago discarded Teddy-bear, resuscitated now because there was no Gina to hug her good night. Her cheeks were wet with tears recently shed. A sudden deep unbidden tenderness overwhelmed him. As he looked at her, he knew that for the first time in his life, he was close to her, linked with her in a shared loss and grief.

He bent and kissed her cheek, tasting the salt of her tears. She stirred, put her arms around his neck and hugged him sleepily, childishly. Very gently, he put her arms back beneath the bedclothes, straightened the pillow, pulled the eiderdown up beneath her chin.

'Good night, darling!'

'Good night, Daddy!'

He tiptoed from the room, tears choking his throat but a strange warm feeling of love for his child slowly melting the icy case around his heart.

The publishers hope that this book has given you enjoyable reading. Large Print Books are especially designed to be as easy to see and hold as possible. If you wish a complete list of our books please ask at your local library or write directly to:

Dales Large Print Books
Magna House, Long Preston,
Skipton, North Yorkshire.
BD23 4ND

This Large Print Book, for people
who cannot read normal print,
is published under the auspices of

THE ULVERSCROFT FOUNDATION

... we hope you have enjoyed this book.
Please think for a moment about those
who have worse eyesight than you ...
and are unable to even read or enjoy
Large Print without great difficulty.

You can help them by sending a
donation, large or small, to:

**The Ulverscroft Foundation,
1, The Green, Bradgate Road,
Anstey, Leicestershire, LE7 7FU,
England.**
or request a copy of our brochure for
more details.

The Foundation will use all donations
to assist those people who are visually
impaired and need special attention
with medical research, diagnosis
and treatment.

Thank you very much for your help.